J Craig

ONE TEAM IN TALLINN

Trafford
PUBLISHING™

Order this book online at www.trafford.com/07-1528
or email orders@trafford.com

Most Trafford titles are also available at major online book retailers.

Note for Librarians: A cataloguing record for this book is available from Library
and Archives Canada at www.collectionscanada.ca/amicus/index-e.html

ISBN: 978-1-4251-3824-0

*We at Trafford believe that it is the responsibility of us all, as both individuals
and corporations, to make choices that are environmentally and socially sound.
You, in turn, are supporting this responsible conduct each time you purchase a
Trafford book, or make use of our publishing services. To find out how you are
helping, please visit www.trafford.com/responsiblepublishing.html*

*Our mission is to efficiently provide the world's finest, most comprehensive
book publishing service, enabling every author to experience success.
To find out how to publish your book, your way, and have it available
worldwide, visit us online at www.trafford.com/10510*

www.trafford.com

North America & international
toll-free: 1 888 232 4444 (USA & Canada)
phone: 250 383 6864 ♦ fax: 250 383 6804
email: info@trafford.com

The United Kingdom & Europe
phone: +44 (0)1865 722 113 ♦ local rate: 0845 230 9601
facsimile: +44 (0)1865 722 868 ♦ email: info.uk@trafford.com

10 9 8 7 6 5 4 3 2 1

To Marjory

Chapter 1

Monarch of the Glen

ATHOLL MCCLACKIT COAXED his Aston Martin up the driveway to Castle McClackit and was struck, once more, by the complete and utter grotesqueness of the place. How his father had such an emotional attachment to this architectural monstrosity was beyond him. It had been in the family since 1745 or at least the land had. A generous present from the grateful Duke of Cumberland to his great-great-great-great grandfather for services rendered in a couple of mopping up operations post Culloden. The Victorian gothic pile that stood before him was a present from Queen Victoria to his great grandfather for services rendered. To think that gillie John Brown copped all the flack for entertaining her majesty when old Rory McClackit had been rodgering her rotten. Outstanding work from the McClackits yet again. He tried to put the image of his great grandfather and the leader of the world's greatest ever Empire going at it hammer and tongs to one side to concentrate on the matter in hand. An urgent summons from his father meant only one thing—bad news for Atholl.

They had struggled on with a strained relationship down the years, not love and hate but more complete and utter frustration with each other for not understanding their respective points of view. The old boy had never been the same since Atholl had pointed out to him he could not simply assassinate Nelson Mandela the moment he stepped out of jail and that sometimes it's better to let things run their course. Father had not seen the logic of this viewpoint and relations had been somewhat strained over the last couple of years. However, his father had been there when needed by Atholl in the past. Atholl would definitely be there for him should any assistance be called for.

He rang the bell at the front door. A few minutes later he was greeted by the sight of his father's faithful retainer, Potter, as the door opened. "Good day master Atholl," came the usual welcome. For once Potter had managed to remove the look of distaste from his face when he addressed Atholl, which immediately put the young master on his guard. Atholl remembered Potter being a helping hand for his father in Kenya in the 1950's as they tore around the country putting down the Mau Mau rebellion with some considerable force. He remembered his father once telling him only to visit Kenya under an assumed name as in some parts of Nairobi to this day, a person of nefarious character was still referred to as a "Emclacket".

As Potter picked up Atholl's bag, another sign all was not well, Atholl thought silence was the best policy and quietly followed him into the hall.

"The chief will see you in his bedroom, sir" announced Potter. So much for the offer of a drink after the long drive thought Atholl.

"I take it he is alone?" inquired Atholl, silently praying his father's latest bit of stuff wouldn't be keeping him company as had happened in the past.

"No sir, he's quite, quite alone but now you're here...." Potter let the sentence trail off. Atholl ignored the irony of Potter's last statement. He had never hidden his dislike of the place and was an infrequent visitor. He climbed the stairs to his father's bedroom walking past the family portraits of earlier chieftains of the clan McClackit. It was an ID parade for those most wanted for crimes against Scotland.

He entered his father's bedroom without knocking, safe in the knowledge his father was on his own. When Atholl was eighteen he'd walked in to the bedroom to see him having sex, doggy style, with the wife of his father's oldest and best friend, the chieftain of the clan McChisholm. It wouldn't have been too bad, apart from the fact his father was dressed as Napoleon at the time which explained a lot of things to Atholl but didn't make the sight any more appealing.

As Atholl approached the bed, his father opened one eye and ceased his furtive hand movements under the sheets. The room was comfortably warm for his father, in other words stiflingly hot for Atholl. His father's love of Africa extended beyond long legged Masai cattle women to the heat of the continent, a warmth he was forever trying to recreate in his bedroom.

"Ah Atholl, excellent to see you. Not quite who I was hoping for, but the need to speak to you, it has to be said, has surpassed certain physical needs that I may have preferred to fulfill."

Atholl had a very clear idea what those needs were and the thought of them made him even more uncomfortable.

"I received your message father and came as soon as I

could manage". This was not strictly true, as a belly dancer in a Lebanese restaurant off the Edgware Road could testify. The night before he'd planned to leave, Atholl had popped out for quick meze only to be waylaid by a pair of gyrating hips as opposed to some freshly made houmus. His large tip of twenty pounds to the waiter had gained him an audience with the dancer, after she finished her set and one thing had led to another. This ended up with him getting some highly detailed and intensive private instruction in pelvic movement back at his house.

His father smiled benevolently at Atholl. "Well done, my boy. Your response is most admirable and you know I would not have summoned you had it not been a matter of great importance. Sit yourself down and I will begin a tale, which, to my great embarrassment, reflects none too well on your father." Dair McClackit attempted to push himself up into a proper sitting position but could only manage a half-hearted shrug of his shoulders. Atholl had to help him up the rest of the way.

Atholl was braced for another tale of vicious Mau Mau suppression or stories of Conservative Party funds siphoned to aid the Smith regime in Rhodesia in the 1970's but the tale was far removed from either of those murky episodes.

His father looked him in the eye, cleared his throat and began. "When I came back from Kenya in the late 50's, I was a caged lion. The army did not want me, after one complaint too many from the High Commissioner in Nairobi. I asked for a transfer to the British Army of the Rhine but that was turned down flat. I was not in a mood to disagree. The thought of spending winter after winter freezing my proverbials on Lunefeld Heath did not appeal greatly. So I came back here and was looking for something to occupy my time, a new direction, a different challenge in life." Dair shook his head, a regretful look on his face.

"Sadly I went back to the old ways of wine, women and song. There were a number of clan chief's daughters I had but you know me, always like a "bit of rough" every now and then to go with the, supposed, "smooth" of the daughters of the cream of Highland society. We had a number of servants in those days, unlike now when Potter is expected to do everything from cook my breakfast to repair the roof." At this point he paused, seemingly lost for a moment in another time, another place. Atholl cleared his throat and his father came back from wherever he'd been.

"One maid in particular caught my eye, Denise Bradley was her name. There was something about her, some hint of defiance just as if she was daring you to try it on. This went on for about a month or so and then it just happened. I literally walked into her one day turning a corner as she was carrying a bundle of freshly ironed sheets. Next thing we're at it like rutting stags. One of those Highland flings I thought at the time but then I just couldn't keep my hands off her. She was just as keen, I should add." At this he paused to pick up a glass of water from his bedside table and take a sip.

"Well, we went at it like mad things for the best part of the summer of 1959. She helped sober me up and made me think about what I wanted to do with my life. She was a great aid at a critical time in my life. I dare say you can guess what happened with all that sex. She fell pregnant. I was happy but concerned about what your grandfather would do to the both of us, so I told her it was over. She would have to leave for the safety of

9

herself and the child." At this the clan chief's voice started to tremble but a quick cough allowed him to gather his thoughts and he continued.

"I offered to pay for an abortion but she wouldn't hear of it. She was determined to keep the child. Given the circumstances, she believed a return home to Dumfries was for the best. I have done a number of terrible things in my life, Atholl. I have killed men with my own bare hands and have gladly taken anything that a time of war and conflict could offer. How do you think this place has been so well maintained? But I have never felt the complete and utter sense of loss as I put Denise on the train at Inverness on that day in 1960. Your own birth two years later was a great consolation. I am proud of the McClackit I see in front of me now."

Atholl was taken aback by his father's words. He had expected some nonsense regarding next year's election and a plan to sabotage the Labour campaign but the conversation had gone off at a tangent and he had no idea where it would end.

"What I have to tell you now, you may have guessed already, is you have a half brother. He was born on the 25th of June 1960 in Dumfries and his name is Kenneth Bradley. I want you to find him and kill him."

"Kill him? I did hear you right, father? You did say kill him?" asked a rather puzzled Atholl. This was not what he had been expecting. At times during the story, his father had actually appeared sentimental, not an emotion one normally associated with the old man and quite a disturbing sight, if truth be told. Atholl was trying to come to terms with what he had just heard. Discovering one had a sibling after all these years was shocking enough, but to be told to kill him left him feeling somewhat numb. He had driven north expecting to listen to a rant from his father relating to the impotence of the Tory government under John Major or a request for some funding to underwrite a white coup in Zimbabwe. Most certainly not an instruction to kill a half brother he had not known existed until five minutes earlier.

"Yes, kill him. I have been experimenting with the trial version of a drug called Ciagra. Some contacts in America managed to procure it for me. It helps to treat a diminished male libido."

Atholl raised an eyebrow.

"Yes, after all this time I have been having difficulty getting the old chap erect. This drug has been marvellous. The McClackit broadsword has been wielded to good effect of late. I've certainly been more active than I have been for a long time. Sally McChisholm is coming over this afternoon as a matter of fact." And is the Napoleon outfit coming out of the wardrobe, wondered Atholl.

From his initial happiness of discussing the effects of the drug, Dair's face darkened.

"Sadly one of the side effects of the drug that they have just discovered is an excessive strain on the heart. This has led to the suspension of the drug trials and my supply is rapidly dwindling. I have been to Inverness for a check up and the prognosis is not good. It's complete rest and recuperation and they might be able to get another 12 months for me. Alternatively, I can live life to the full for another few months and take my chances. As I said, Sally is coming over so you can guess which option I have taken. Therefore Atholl, within the next couple of years you will become chief of the clan McClackit. It must be a sole claim on the title and no other individual's claim must be possible. Am I making myself clear?" This last question was spoken in crisper, clearer tones than any other.

"Crystal clear, father, absolutely crystal clear" replied Atholl. "I will need a bit of time to think this through but be assured, I will not let you down. Are you absolutely certain he has to be killed? It is quite conceivable he has no knowledge at all of his claim the to the title."

"That is completely correct, dear boy. He might have no idea but I am fully aware of his mother's knowledge. She was no fool and I let her down very, very badly. If she saw it as a way of getting back at me and the clan, she could make him lay a claim to the title and we would be in a legal battle that could cost thousands and prevent you from taking up your rightful inheritance."

Atholl was about to suggest it might be easier to kill the mother but he did not want to put anymore strain on his father's heart. The heat in the room had suddenly become completely unbearable for him and he stood up to try and open a window for a cooling draught. His father twitched in frustration as the temperature dropped but was powerless to prevent Atholl letting in some fresh air.

At this point, Atholl sensed the meeting with his father had gone on long enough. It was a shock to the system to discover in one breath you had a half brother, then in the next sentence, to be told by your father, the father to you both incidentally, that you should kill him. He went over to the bed, shook his father's hand and walked out of the bedroom.

He walked down the stairs in time to see Potter open the front door and let in Sally McChisholm. She must have been in her late fifties by now but was still extremely attractive. She reminded him of a Highland version of Marianne Faithful.

Sally McChisholm looked up the stairs at the sound of Atholl's footsteps.

"Atholl? I haven't seen you since you were teenager, dear boy. I expect you don't recognise me with my clothes on". At this Atholl blushed. Good God, he thought, don't these elderly types have any shame?

"I'd recognise you anywhere Mrs McChisholm" he replied.

"It's Sally to you, dear boy. Just been to see your father?"

"Yes I have."

"Is le petit general on good form?"

"Mais oui" replied Atholl

"Excellent" answered Sally "I hope we shall have the chance to catch up later, once I am finished with your father." She gave him a knowing look and started to walk up the stairs. He couldn't be sure, but when she was halfway up, he thought he vaguely heard an "Au revoir," waft down from above.

Atholl wandered into his father's study on the ground floor. His father's desk was positioned so whoever sat there could look out of the large bay window onto a large garden. Atholl plonked himself down in his father's chair and twirled about for a bit, trying to come to terms with what the old boy had said. As he sat pondering his father's orders he thought he heard the strains of the 1812 Overture being played somewhere. He thought it must be drifting up from the kitchen where Potter might have the radio on. He picked up his father's ivory paper opener, yet another Kenyan souvenir he presumed, and pressed the point against the ball of his thumb. He needed to try and understand how he came to be dragged back into such a position by his father. Would he ever be free of the McClackit name and all its baggage? He suddenly realised he'd drawn blood on his thumb, he'd been pressing so hard. He stood up. If he couldn't be free of the name he could certainly be free of the castle. He didn't care that he'd just arrived, he'd get back on the road and maybe stop off in Moffat or the Lakes. Another moment in this place would do nothing to improve his state of mind.

He went looking for Potter. He found him in the kitchen watching a football match on TV. He seemed somewhat agitated for him and Atholl was intrigued to see this insight into a man who had remained completely cool and distant from him.

"Good game, Potter?" asked Atholl.

"Naw, complete shite, if you must know" came the reply. Potter suddenly realised to whom he was talking, "Sorry Master Atholl, was a bit caught up there. It's England v Scotland at Wembley. McAllister has just missed a penalty."

"Oh yes, who for?" asked Atholl feigning an interest in a game he knew nothing about.

"Scotland" came a somewhat muted reply. Potter failing completely to keep the look of bemusement at the young arsehole in front of him from his face.

They were both looking at the TV as a player in a white top lobbed a player in dark blue to score a second goal for England with a peach of a volley. "Aw, fuck" went Potter. Taking this as the final cue to leave, Atholl tried to re-assert his authority.

"Potter, will you inform my father, once he is, eh, free, I have decided to get on with his request straight away and as such, I am leaving immediately. I will contact him once I have accomplished what he requested"

"Ok, Master Atholl. I am sure he will look forward to hearing from you" came the reply. Potter was still staring at the TV, a disappointed look on his face.

Atholl thought he could still hear the sound of the 1812 Overture from somewhere.

"Do you have a radio anywhere in the kitchen, Potter?" he asked

"No sir, the only radio is in the car" said Potter a slightly amused look on his face.

"You can't hear any music then?" asked Atholl.

"No sir, the only thing I can hear is your voice" a smile playing on his lips.

Atholl felt he'd somehow missed a joke at his expense.

"Very well. I'll say cheerio Potter and thank you for all your help"

"Anytime Master Atholl, anytime sir. I'll just get your bag" said Potter happy in the knowledge that if the football was buggered, at least Atholl was leaving the building.

Atholl reached the Dunblane roundabout just north of Stirling in good time. On the drive down he'd been thinking back to his time in the army and how his career had mirrored his father's earlier military career of the 1950's. They'd both been involved in brutally suppressing insurgent terrorists in differing areas. His father in Kenya and he in Northern Ireland. They'd both had difficulty coming to terms with civilian life but in his, Atholl's case, he'd been able to temper the disappointment of civvy street with his job. Their military background had left each of them accepting the loss of life but single minded in the realisation of what might have to be sacrificed in an attempt to achieve one's objectives. In the army, Atholl had been a one-man campaign against lawlessness in Northern Ireland until he had, even by his own admission, got a bit carried away. Had his father not got in touch with him and told him to stop, he thought he would still be terrorising the terrorists in the six counties. That phone call had made a tremendous difference to him, finally bringing him to his senses over what he was doing with his career and his life. The old boy had spoken from the heart, he'd been in the same position himself so he knew what he was talking about. Atholl had known his time in Ulster would come to an end one day and had taken similar precautions to those of his father in Kenya.

Shortly before he withdrew back to the mainland he'd discovered the IRA were brokering a cocaine deal with sympathisers in New York who had contacts with Colombians in Miami. He'd been able to intercept the couriers taking the money back to the States when they attempted to return to Knock in the south. Their cover was a religious pilgrimage from the States and they hoped no one would notice the small matter of them carrying five million dollars cash back into the USA.

Atholl had always known his nun's habit would come in handy sometime. He had followed the main man of the two into a gents in a Little Chef, pretending to be a poorly sighted nun. The poor guy had been totally unprepared for Atholl sticking a knife in his jugular whilst protesting in high pitched voice that they really should make the signs on the doors a lot clearer. He had dragged the body into a cubicle and knew it would only be a matter of time before the second of the two came looking. When he turned up, the end result had been pretty much the same. Atholl had left the two bodies, one sitting on top of each other, in the cubicle. He'd changed out of the habit and put it into a bag he'd hidden under the robes. Having relieved one of the bodies of their car keys, he then proceeded to drive to Fishguard for the ferry to Wales and a new life amongst the great unwashed of British civilians.

Now, as he passed the looming rock of Stirling Castle he realised the mistake his father had made and one he wasn't keen to repeat. Neither of them had come to terms with the fact they were no longer at war. Peacetime was played by different rules, yet nobody set the rules when it came to the McClackits, apart from the clan members themselves. However, everybody handled things differently and Atholl was determined his own actions would not be handicapped by the legacy of the history of the McClackits. At the same time, he realised he could not easily escape the responsibility of his father's command. Family duty before all else was better, he concluded.

Following on from this decision, Atholl attempted to rationalise the demands his father had made on him with the resources it would require to complete the job in hand. He understood the impossibility, of the task as he had no information regarding his quarry. How would he find out who this person was, where he lived, indeed if he was still alive, and what type of life he was leading now? He suddenly realised this might not be quite as easy as his father thought.

Chapter 2

———

Early Doors

IT WAS AN oppressive July day in Glasgow, sultry hot with low cloud cover. The pub opposite Queen Street station had air conditioning of a sort, an open window, but this was soon closed when an OAP who had been nursing a half of lager for approximately three hours complained of a draught. The heat in the pub due to the climatic conditions was one thing but the hot air emissions from one of the drinkers was another.

"Brazilians? Don't get me stertit on those pricks. Patronisin', arrogant bastarts the lot o them. Sexy samba soccer, stick it up yer arse, like. Ah've seen those yellow-shirted tossers play in 3 World Cups and ah hate them. They're more fucken arrogant than the Germans or the French, like. Look, the ones you see at the World Cups, where have they come fae? The slums o' Rio? Ah don't think so. They're either students studyin in Europe ie rich bastarts or they can afford to fly over from Brazil for the tournament ie even richer bastarts." The rant halted for a quick lager break.

"Ah was sittin at that game in Seville in 1982, like. We go 4-1 down when the boy behind me hits us on the shoulder, no in a friendly way either, and goes "Hey Scotland, that is how you play football". A true statement, fair enough but no one ah really wanted to hear at that moment in time. He was sittin wi a crackin burd, mind. But ye look at those scenes outside the ground in Seville, are the Brazilians samba-in wi the Tartan Army? Are they fuck! And then there's all these sad Scots pricks wearin Brazil tops wi their kilts. Exactly what do we have in common wi those cunts? They're a debt ridden third world country wi a tropical climate, we're a debt ridden third world country wi a crap climate. Ma taxes have paid for those bastarts to get to the World Cup and all ah get is fuckin' patronised. Well make no mistake pal, the next time we play those cunts ah won't be there, that's for fucken certain".

"So its fair to say you're no that keen on the boys from Brazil?" asked Kenny

"Ye could say that,."replied Gus.

Kenny Bradley watched his pal, Gus McSween, and wondered where it all came from. He'd only got to know him that well in 1979 and seventeen years later he was still discovering new things about him. Their friendship had been forged on a trip to Oslo for the Norway v Scotland game. Scotland had won 4-0 and even more incredibly, Kenny had saved Gus's life by persuading two Marines from the US Embassy in Oslo not to tear Gus limb from limb after he had sung, non stop for 15 minutes , to the tune of Guantanamera, "One Viet Cong, there's only one Viet Cong" in the Highlander bar.

They had been firm friends ever since but even Kenny had not realised the bile stored up in Gus regarding Brazilians. How can five foot nothing of flabby Scotsman possess such complete and utter hatred of Brazilians, Tenby, farmers and the Wimbledon tennis tournament?

"Whit's the jackanory aboot Vienna then?" asked Gus.

"No problem, if you can actually find your way to cough up some cash for the flights and the hotel." replied Kenny.

"Aye ok, ah'll write you a cheque the now"

"A cheque?" coughed Kenny. "When the fuck did you get a chequebook? What bank manager was stupid enough to give you one?"

"Easy tiger" came the reply. "After ma gas and electricity gettin cut off ah thought ah'd better screw the nut and concentrate on gettin my fiscal matters in hand, like. So, ah've opened up a new bank account and am workin ma way towards a positive financial outlook on life. Ah've even been thinkin about investin in a PEP"

"But your gas and electricity are still cut off" pointed out Kenny

"Hey, its central heatin or this trip to Vienna, ye've got ta get yer priorities right".

"Fair enough" agreed Kenny.

Kenny and Gus stood at the bar. Kenny had just left the Glasgow Film Theatre having watched Godfather Parts 1 and 2 on a double bill. He had the videos at home but nothing compared to the big screen as far as he was concerned. He'd offered to take his friend along but Gus was rooted to the bar.

Scotland were beginning their World Cup qualifying campaign for France 98 in Austria in a eight weeks time so Gus was getting in some pre match drinking practice. As ever, despite the fact he had put away a minimum of six pints of Tennents lager in the time Kenny had been in the cinema, the wee man was not showing any signs of being the worse for wear.

"Ah think the Austrians have had a bad deal over the years, like. Why should the actions of one person who just happened to be born on their soil, damn them to the end of eternity?" said Gus, a philosophical tone entering his voice, now his rant was finished.

"You mean Hitler?" asked Kenny wanting to see how far a stupid question would push his little fat friend.

"No, Baron Von Trapp ya muppet!" exploded Gus. "Of course ah mean Hitler. What other Austrian's been responsible for the death of millions and a world war?"

"Forgive me if I am missing something here but how did we get from Austria to your anti-Brazilian rant?" enquired Kenny

"The Odessa File, ye said ye'd been watchin it on TV the other night, Jon Voight and that dark haired bird wi the big jugs that also appeared in the Likely Lads film," replied Gus.

"Ah yes, and I'd made the mistake of saying how I never understood how many Nazis actually made it to Brazil. Of course, how forgetful of me," mused Kenny as he tried to work out how such an innocent question could provoke such unbridled fury. The opening bars of Wonderwall sung by Oasis began to waft across the bar. Gus perked up at the sound of the song.

"Too right, today is goin to be the day, ma man. Got an appointment with the financial adviser later on like. You may have noticed ah'm a bit smarter dressed than normal, like. Dress to impress, if you get my drift," said Gus with a certain note of pride in his voice.

"Please don't tell me it's a woman," said Kenny giving Gus

a once over to see what exactly he had done to improve on his dress sense. Working in a white collar job as a union rep in the finance industry, Gus had better than average taste in clothes. He was normally a fastidious, if conservative, dresser. His clothes were clean and his shirts always ironed but one or two personal quirks tended to lessen the overall sartorial effect. In this case, his buckled, cuban heeled cowboy boots which were cut off at the ankles.

"How many times have I told you not to wear those bloody awful boots? And with chinos! People with a complex about their height wear those. Oh sorry, I've just realised I am talking to a five foot tall Scotsman, so I apologise for stating the truth so bluntly. For fuck's sake, she's going to take one look at those and think they're cut off boots for a cut off guy."

Gus squirmed uncomfortably in the corner. He had gone for the boots as a last resort. He'd only spoken to the girl, what was her name, Fiona or Maria, after the teller in the bank suggested he might want to meet a financial adviser to ensure his long term financial goals were attainable. He hadn't been keen and when he told the teller his short term financial goals were getting his gas and electricity re-connected, the wee laddie had looked a bit abashed, to put it mildly. When the kid had pointed out she'd only take half an hour of his time, Gus had perked up. A she. This was better than Dateline, it was free and she had to talk to you. Ya beauty. He'd been having a few drinks to give him a wee confidence boost but nothing too over the top.

"Ok, maybe they werenae the right choice but ah don't know how tall she is, like. Ah don't want to feel she's dominating me into takin out a pension or an endowment mortgage. Anyway, forget aboot that the now. What's the Hampden roar about this double header then? Riga and Tallinn! Does it get any better?" said Gus trying to regain some control of the situation.

"You havenae heard the price of the flights yet." Kenny replied, an element of frustration creeping into his voice. "I've been looking at a domino ticket. I don't know why they call it that but we can fly with SAS from Edinburgh to Copenhagen then from Copenhagen to Riga and on the way back Tallinn to Copenhagen and Copenhagen to Edinburgh. We've only got to make our own way from Riga to Tallinn but I am sure we can get a bus or a train or something. I'm definitely up for it but what about you?" replied Kenny who was wondering just what the wee man was going to do for funds to pay for the double header trip. It sounded a belter. A few folk might be put off by the expense, especially after it came so soon after the Austria away game but a trip to the Baltics was unmissable.

Gus looked thoughtful. "There are some things in life that are not to be missed so ah'll get the money together somehow. The fanny in Tallinn is worth the cost of any flight, like," was his reply.

"So given that this financial adviser is hardly going to be swayed by the state of your finances, what do you expect to come of this meeting?" he asked Gus.

"I don't know, to be honest but if ah can get her to come out on a date it will be a cheap one for me, that's for certain," Gus replied, a gleeful smile playing on his lips.

"Are there any other kind for you?" replied Kenny, a mischievous look on his face.

"Ha fuckin ha. Once she's seen my personal books she'll know ahm right in the financial clag, so to speak, like. So, if we go out for a meal, she's goin to have to cough for her share as she'll know ah've no got the cash. Then again she can get a full dividend from ma bounteous loins later on, if it all goes to plan. She'll maybe take a deposit from my sperm bank, if ye catch my drift. Ah'll definitely be giving her a special rate of interest, like." Gus rubbed his hands together in anticipation.

"So how are you going to explain the hair transplant loan?" asked Kenny.

"Shut the fuck up about that, people might hear ye," pleaded Gus, a hurt look on his face.

"Fuck off, people with impaired vision can see that bit of turf has been stitched on to your scalp. It wouldnae be so bad but its also ginger. Whatever possessed you?"

This had been an ongoing argument for the last three months since Gus, in a fit of depression due to the ending of another relationship, had become convinced women didn't respect him, due to his baldness.

In his eyes, his complete disinterest in a woman once he'd had sexual intercourse with her was not an issue. Nor was his continual lateness, should they go out for an evening. Nor his complete and utter disinterest in any part of that woman's life. His lack of interest in joint holidays had also been a handicap in his attempts to forge strong relationships with numerous girlfriends. The last nail in his relationship coffin, the fact they were barred from his away trips supporting the Scotland football team, hardly enamoured him to a few either.

One previous girlfriend had made the mistake of giving him an ultimatum after they'd just had sex. Standing over Gus as she was hooking her bra on she started on him, "It's a trip to Yugoslavia to see that useless shower of bastards called Scotland or it's me. You've had my last words on the subject". Gus hardly helped matters by then asking her if she could iron a couple of shirts for him while he looked for his passport. Another one bit the dust.

Gus had regretted the transplant, but it was too late. He'd been influenced by the freak of nature that was his goatee beard. Trying to look trendy, he had grown a goatee only to find it had come out ginger in direct contrast to the remaining hair on his head which was dark brown. He hadn't fancied the ginger effect until he thought one girl in a nightclub told him he looked like Frank MacAvennie, a footballer whose reputation as a Casanova knew no limits. Gus had taken this as a compliment even though the girl had actually said "rank fanny" as opposed to, "Frank MacAvennie". Gus had forgotten all about MacAvennie's ginger pubes reputation and had gone on to get the hair transplant done in bright ginger. Some cruel soul once said his scalp now looked like Rannoch Moor in autumn except more windswept..

"Look, ah know it's not perfect but get off ma back. Ahm carryin an injury as well, like." he replied.

"Injury? Just how the fuck are you injured?" Kenny replied.

"Ah've got a bit of a cold, like." At this Gus sniffed, just to complete the effect.

"But its' July. How the fuck do you get a cold in July, ignoring the fact we are in the middle of a typical Scottish summer?" Kenny was getting bit worked up by now as was often the case when he spent more than 30 minutes in one to one contact with Gus.

"The duvet cover was a bit damp when ah put it back on, like. Ah think I've got a chill," muttered Gus in a low tone.

"Am I right in thinking from you saying this you only have one set of bed linen?" said Kenny in an equally low voice.

"Aye, that's right. How did ye guess? How many sets o' linen do you have, like?"

"Three," replied Kenny

"Whats the point in havin three, ya daft cunt?" This reply was accompanied by a big smirk from Gus.

"Because then I don't get a cold through being forced to put my one set of damp bedding back on the fucking bed, you thick muppet." shouted Kenny. "No wonder you can't maintain a relationship. What a chat up line "Would like to come back to my place and roll about in some damp sheets?" Fuck me, it would be like shagging Fungus the Bogeyman. When are you ever going to get a grip on reality?"

Gus was not amused by Kenny having a go. He was trying to get in a good mood for meeting this financial adviser and here he was winding him up like a cheap watch.

"Look here, pal, we dinnae all have bed linen comin out of our ears or time to worry about how tae iron a fitted sheet." In a moment of drunken madness Kenny had once complained to Gus about the difficulty in getting a good iron on fitted bedsheets, how the elasticated edgings were a nightmare to get straight on the ironing board. He had regretted it ever since.

"Most of the time you sit on yer arse trying to avoid pickin up customers in that taxi of yours," moaned Gus who was rapidly losing the plot through a combination of drink and nerves at the blind date or rather, finanancial consultation, coming up in twenty minutes.

"Hey lads, let's keep it down a bit". Kenny and Gus turned

to the bar where Alex the barman was holding out his hands, palm downwards in a placatory gesture.

"Oops, sorry about that Alex," said Kenny, "got a bit carried away with the ginger ninja here".

"Ach, shut it, you" replied Gus. "No problem Alex, ahm just off to meet my date anyway. Ah'll speak to you later," he said to Kenny, wagging a finger in his face.

Gus was halfway to the door when Alex shouted to him "Wait minute Gus, there's a question I've got for you"

Gus turned and walked back to the bar, "What is it big man? Glad you've asked somebody with a bit o' intelligence, unlike some o' yer customers here", at this he shot a venomous glance in the direction of Kenny.

"Ah've always wondered" said Alex ,"how did so many Germans end up in Brazil at the end of the war?"

Chapter 3

Executive Decision

ATHOLL WAS SURPRISED how swiftly the meeting with the private detective was concluded. He hadn't expected the detective to be a female or quite so businesslike. He had thought of asking if she'd like to see his private dick but thought better of it when she'd let it drop into the conversation, ever so casually, she was a black belt at judo. She viewed his request for all the personal details of Kenneth Bradley with barely concealed contempt, promising him a complete report in a week. When he'd asked if it would include photographs, the reply that photos would delay the report arriving for another week and would cost an extra 150 pounds. This had given him a chance to flex his financial muscle, "Make it £250 but they must arrive before the end of the week". This had appeared to impress the young lady but not enough for her to accept his offer of a drink in the Atlantic Bar. Oh well, she was a bit on the tall side anyway, so no real loss.

As he thought about his father, he wondered if Kenneth Bradley was the only half brother or even sister he had. There had been rumours in the family that when it came to sex, his father had been in the same mould as Rory the Rodgerer. If he'd screwed so many women, was it possible there were only two children sired? As ever, Atholl took the objective approach and realised there was no point in worrying about something he could neither qualify nor quantify. The main issue at the moment was, who was Kenneth Bradley and how much of a threat, if any, he posed to the clan McClackit? As he gazed out his office window at the Thames, he realised that stiff action might be called for. He'd done it before, he could do it again. When the report arrived at the end of the week, Atholl had expected a bit more for his money. He had been used to military files in the past where every scrap of information, however useless, had been included. The private detective's report seemed to be very basic, giving one little or no sense of feel about the man himself.

Atholl had scanned the skimpy personal details and decided to concentrate on the photos. So my half-brother is a Glasgow taxi driver, he thought as he looked at the photo of a medium-sized guy climbing into the driving seat of a black cab. Married with no children, wife's name is Alison and he is normally known as Kenny. He looks a bit older than he is with a receding hairline, brushed back hair with a few streaks of grey, thought Atholl. Degree in Film and Media Studies from Stirling University but living in a flat in a part of Glasgow called Hyndland. Atholl had always believed the home and where it was said a lot about the individual. It was not always true, as he had met some Belfast drug barons worth a mint, who had lived in a beautiful house in the middle of a council estate, but those were extreme cases. He picked up his phone and spoke to his PA. "Carol, speak to the property department would you please. Ask them to get me a valuation on a two bedroom flat in Hyndland, Glasgow. Could I have it as soon as? Thanks."

Five minutes later his phone rang and Carol duly informed Atholl that a two bedroom flat in Hyndland would be worth somewhere in the region of 100,000 pounds but selected areas could be £150,000 plus. This made Atholl think. The black cab work in Glasgow couldn't be as lucrative as it was in London. What did his wife do? Part time accounts work for a souvenir company on the south side of the city. I suppose if you put both salaries together, it might work out, given they had no kids, but something didn't seem quite right.

No kids, eh? They were both in their mid thirties, the clock was ticking for her, so where were the rugrats? The way things were going there would be no heirs to the McClackit title from either of them. Atholl had been married once, a lovely girl called Fiona. He had sometimes wondered where it had all gone wrong but the answer to that was simple. Coming home to find your wife in bed with two members of the New Zealand women's netball team was where it all went a little sour. Fiona had thought the issue could be solved by asking him to join the three of them for a little fun and games but it was too little, too late. They'd both been open minded with regards to their relationship but this was a step too far, especially as he had been coming home early to discuss with her the production of a little McClackit of their own.

Had he been hasty? He would never know but it was all water under the bridge now. Fiona had left their marital home shortly after the episode with the Kiwis and he believed she was now in Baja California, helping an old friend run a boutique hotel that catered to the special needs of Hollywood stars. He had a very clear idea of what those requirements were as he had visited the hotel once with Fiona. One night the pair of them had ended up in a hot tub orgy, the most famous participant being an extremely coked out River Phoenix. Special needs indeed.

Getting back to the matter in hand, Atholl felt he had been short changed by the detective agency. In terms of general information there was little or nothing, no details of personal interests, friendships or the casual dross which is part and parcel of a normal life. He needed background info if he was going to get to know his target and this was just not good enough. Atholl picked up the phone to call the lady he'd met a week earlier and this time he would be asking for a little more than Kenny Bradley's name and bloody address.

* * * * *

Kenny sat in his cab outside Central Station. He'd been up since the crack of dawn trying to work up some funds for the trip to Vienna. The morning wasn't his best time of the day. His mood had hardly been helped the night before when Alison had burst out laughing as he told her what he was planning to do.

"You're meant to be supportive," he'd pointed out to her once she'd regained a bit of composure. "I thought it says in all those women's mags that a relationship is a mutually supportive organism, each individual helps the other to achieve their goals in life for the mutual benefit of the relationship as a whole".

"Aye, but where does it say your lazy arsehole of a husband is going to get out of bed at 6am for the first time in his life in an effort to drum up the fare to Vienna? If Craig Brown knew you were doing this you'd be in the squad. I've told you, if you

31

need the spends I'll give you some cash, it's not an issue." She reached for her handbag, prepared to pull out her purse. "In fact why don't you wake up early and stay in bed to give me a nice wee early wake up call? Eh? It'll be a real treat going into work with a smile on my face for once."

Although tempted, Kenny had been feeling more guilty than normal recently with regards to living off his wife. Gus' crack about the ironing had needled him more than he had let on, so he had told Alison he was going to try and do something for himself for once. He appreciated her offer but work was work. He wasn't going to let the chance of a fly midweek shag get in his way.

It was 7.30 am and he was first in line outside the station, anticipating a nice wee trip to Parkhead industrial estate or even Bishopbriggs. The back door opened and the voice said, "STV studios at Cowcaddens Kenny and don't spare the horses".

Kenny turned round at the directions to face long time friend and Scotland fan, "Cammy, you bastard. I've been waiting for a fare for fifteen minutes and now you just want to go round the corner."

"Sorry, but is the customer not always right? You've got to accept the fare or I'll be reporting you to the city authorities. Now my good man, less of your proletarian lip or there will be no tip".

"You lazy poof" quipped Kenny. "I thought you would have been interested in a bit of walking to keep the weight down."

"Poof yes, lazy no. I got more than enough exercise last night I can tell you. That's why I am, literally, too shagged out to walk up to the studios. Well, that and a need to meet up with the rest of the mincing queers in that place and sort their lives out. For fuck's sake, how do they expect homos to get on in life if a broken finger nail results in a cab ride to A + E accompanied by all and sundry? It's hard being a man's man in a gay man's world."

"Still supporting the Gers?" asked Kenny.

"I am that. That's what's done me for Scotland games. Used to be, in Europe you had a couple of away trips before you got knocked out by Christmas, the rest of the season you could concentrate on Scotland, but the fucker who came up with this Champion's League group qualifying stage wasnae a big club and country fan."

"Not a problem I am ever likely to suffer with," said Kenny.

"Aye, the only Queens in Europe are me, myself, I.

Kenny pondered on this. "You must get some good trips though?"

"You can only take Derry's Walls being screamed at some peasant girl in the middle of the steppes, so many times. The meatheads that crawl out from under those stones in Belfast leave a bit to be desired, though there's some quality shagging to be done on these trips"

"No way," said Kenny. "You always boast you're the only gay Rangers fan in the world."

"I never said fellow "Sons of William" were getting in on the act, it's the rugged manly type in these far off places that just can't get enough or give enough. Many a good night to be had in the depths of the Athens' gay scene, I can tell you," replied Cammy.

"So how is it going with the 38 club?" asked Kenny, a big smile on his face.

"If that question refers to my attempt to have sex with a male supporter of every football team in Scotland, it's going not too bad. Just as well I did an Aberdeen fan in the early days as its pure hatred with the sheep shaggers nowadays. Put a Raith Rovers notch on the bedpost last Saturday after a wee trip to Starks Park. The gents at Kirkcaldy bus station at six o'clock on a Saturday night would put a San Francisco sauna to shame. I've still to crack it with a Queen of the South fan, though Kenny. Funny how men can love Queens but not be homos, eh? Any time you get sick of the lovely Alison, you've got my number."

"There's no chance of that. Can you just imagine Harold's reaction if she went and told him I've left her for a poof?"

Kenny looked in the rear view mirror just in time to see Cammy grimace.

"Point taken. I don't think he would approach the matter in calm and rational manner. Most likely he'd come at it with a blow torch in one hand and chisel in the other."

Kenny turned the taxi into the entrance of the STV studios at Cowcaddens. "Got change of a 50 pound note?" asked Cammy.

"You have got to be joking" said Kenny.

"Ach, keep your pubic hair on, just a wee wind up. There's a tenner for taking you from your spot. You can buy me a drink wi the change the next time I see you. You going to Vienna?

"Aye, why do you think I'm up at this time? I'm looking for all the big tippers".

"Well, have a good time and if you ever meet a gay Queens fan, point them in my direction as I've only three clubs to go".

"Does that include Celtic?" asked Kenny.

"Yes, I still can't find it in my heart of hearts to shag a Tim. Bit of a moral dilemma and that's a first for me. If it's male and got a pulse it's in with a chance but squinty eyed fenians are another story. Enjoy Austria."

Cammy shut the cab door and trotted up the stairs at the front of the studios.

Kenny watched him disappear through the doors and wondered about the chances the mad bastard was taking, going to Europe with Rangers and then looking to pull guys. Oh well, each to their own. As he was wondering what to do for his next fare, his mobile phone went off. He was amazed it was actually ringing. He rarely used it and very few people actually knew the number. One reason for this was Kenny wasn't actually sure of the number himself so was unable to inform anyone who might want to call him. The phone had been a Christmas present from Alison and, but for that, Kenny would have binned it months ago. He picked the phone up but was struggling to remember how to answer the call. He finally pressed the button with the little green phone on it and spoke, very slowly, into the phone. "He-llo, Ke-nny he-er."

The voice of his father-in-law came ringing through the earpiece, "Never mind the phone's batteries, are your batteries runnin down or somethin, ya daft cunt! Why don't ye speak up, ah can hardly hear ye."

Kenny was frozen in his seat. A number of questions ran through his head. Why does Harold MacMillan want to speak to me? How did he get my number? What could be so urgent that he's called me on the mobile? Is Alison ok? The last question seemed the most reasonable to begin with so he remembered to speed up and blurted out "IsAlisonalright?"

"Aye, calm down for fuck's sake. She was awright two minutes ago when she handed me yer number, if that's what ye want tae know."

"Oh thank God for that!" exclaimed Kenny. His palpitations

had subsided but then picked up again when he realised Harold was still on the line. Kenny had good reason to be scared. He had unknowingly married into the MacMillan criminal dynasty, who ruled the south side of Glasgow with an iron fist in an armour plated glove. He loved his wife dearly but a little bit of warning regarding what he was getting into wouldn't have gone unnoticed. How could a sweet wee Glasgow girl whose main interests in life were accountancy, sex and interior design, normally in that order, have sprung from the loins of such a fruit and nut case?

"Where are ye?" came the question in a quieter tone.

"Just outside the STV studios," said Kenny, regaining control of his voice.

"Well, put a fare on the meter tae Pollok Golf Club. Come tae the front entrance and ask fur me. They'll show you intae the member's bar where ah'll be waitin." Harold cut the call and the phone went dead.

Kenny wondered what the problem was. Sorry, should that be opportunity? He'd read somewhere about a management style, somewhere in the States, where there were no problems, only opportunities. Aye but I bet they were never on the wrong side of Michael "Harold" MacMillan which could involve a fucking feast of "opportunities".

Harold's physical similarity to the Conservative Prime Minister of the 1950's was purely coincidental in that they both had grey hair and a bushy moustache. Admittedly, the ministerial Harold MacMillan never looked like some 1970's porn star, unlike his father in law, nobody ever being brave enough to tell him that a feather cut and a Zapata moustache went out with the Raleigh Chopper. Alison once told him her dad had a head of pure jet black hair until he was hit by an arrow from a crossbow. The arrow shot had resulted in a glancing blow causing him to lose his eye. His hair went grey virtually overnight, after he'd lost his eye. Well, losing an eye was one thing but Kenny had never thought or dared to ask about the fate of the archer who had fired the arrow. The southside of Glasgow was not the merrie olde England of Robin Hood but he could imagine a suitably medieval fate had awaited him.

Kenny put the cab in gear and headed off in the direction of Pollok golf club. He'd never planned on being a taxi driver and definitely not in Glasgow. He'd grown up in Dumfries with no fixed plans or interests apart from football, football and more football. It might have helped if he'd been any good at the game but being a competent amateur right back was never going to see him parading his skills at the San Siro.

Kenny had actually become a taxi driver due to Harold MacMillan. He'd been unemployed when he'd got married, a situation that had not caused him or his wife any problems but it had not reflected well on Harold. After the ceremony, Harold had called him and Alison into a little ante room in the hotel where the reception was being held. He told them he was very happy for them both and wanted to give them their present. He'd handed Kenny an envelope which had a substantial object in it. Kenny had opened the envelope to discover a Glasgow taxi drivers badge.

"What does this mean?" Kenny had asked.

"It's yer passport tae a new career, Kenny. Nae son in law o' mine is goin tae be unemployed," said Harold. "Looks like ye've just got yersel a job which allows ye to be really good at what ye do best, sit on yer arse all day."

"But Harold, I can't drive" had been the reply.

"Whit?! Ah've spent ten grand on a taxi licence for ye and ye cannae fucken drive" Harold erupted.

"Calm down dad. It's just his idea of a joke. He can drive, he's just to lazy too do it normally. Thanks, it's a great present" Alison interceded.

Harold visibly calmed down. At one stage Kenny thought his false eye was going to pop out but Kenny's brand new wife had saved his bacon. Oh no, I'm owing her already thought Kenny.

"Fuckin magic. Ah've just let a wind up merchant marry ma daughter. It just gets better and better. Ah'm away for a drink". Harold had walked out of the room and into the reception area.

Kenny pulled into the car park at Pollok Golf Club. As he passed the main sign on his way in some wag had sprayed over the first o in Pollok with a vertical line topped off with a dot. This summed up Kenny's attitude to golfers, a right bunch of pilloks. He'd tried it a couple of times in his younger days at the Royal Dumfries but his fellow junior golfers had been less than welcoming and the less said about the seniors the better. A good walk spoiled indeed.

As he parked the cab and walked up to the entrance he suddenly remembered the story of Harold's trick on the first tee when he was wanting to put his opponent off. Harold would tee up his ball and then step back. He would ask his opponent if he knew why Harold was such a good golfer. If the other player said he didn't know, Harold would take his glass eye out and roll it up to where his ball was teed up. "It's cos ah always keep mah eye on the ball." This normally did the trick in putting the opposition right off their game but Harold had been forced to put an end to it one day. He had not realised the greenkeepers had given the tees a light sprinkling of fertiliser first thing. He'd put his eye back in following the trick, only to have to make a hasty withdrawal to the local A + E to get treatment for inflamation of the optical nerve after double bogeying the third hole. As he was led into an ambulance, he was heard to utter the immortal words "This isnae a fucking forfeit, ah'll be back as soon as they've washed my eye."

He mentioned Harold's name to the old boy at the door and was ushered into a huge clubroom. There were three large bay windows looking out onto the 18th green. A large bar stretched down the opposite side of the room, backed by a gantry which appeared to house just about every whisky in the world, from what Kenny could make out. Harold sat in a leather armchair in one of the bay windows talking to a guy who looked in his late 50's, roughly the same age as Harold but with both eyes fully functional, no doubt.

"Hello Kenny," said Harold as Kenny approached the table. The other man turned round and stood up with his hand outstretched. They shook hands and he introduced himself.

"Hello Kenny, Brian MacDowall. I was just leaving, so apologies at disappearing so quickly. Ok, Harold, I'll be in touch about the matter we were discussing."

Kenny immediately realised this was a man to reckon with, as Harold didn't normally allow people use his nickname in public, unless they were particularly close to him. Kenny used it as he knew it got on Harold's nerves but this was the first time he'd heard someone use it who wasn't a known member of Harold's inner circle.

"Sit doon Kenny. Ah'd offer ye a drink but ah know yer drivin," said Harold with a smile on his face.

"They don't serve non alcoholic drinks here then?" asked Kenny with a mock disappointed look on his face.

"Alright smart bastart. D'ye want a coffee?" grunted Harold.

"No, it's ok. I'm fine" came the reply. Kenny sat down just across from Harold. "What did you want to see me about?" asked Kenny, hoping the note of fear in his voice didn't come out too strongly.

"These two games comin up in October wi Scotland. They're playin Estonia and somebody else, Latvia is it?"

"Aye, Latvia first in Riga and then Estonia in Tallinn. What about them? You know as much about football as I do about golf ie hee haw" Kenny was extremely puzzled by Harold's question and did not anticipate his next comment.

"Very good, ah'm goin tae them"

"You're what?" Kenny sat bolt upright. "You cannot be serious, Harold! You hate football."

Harold looked at Kenny for a moment, a smile playing on his lips, and then said "Ye're right but there's somethin else. Ah've made a business contact in Tallinn and ah'm goin to pay him a wee visit. Thought ah'd hook up wi you and ye can show me the ropes, Tartan Army style."

"Where did you meet a business contact in Tallinn?" asked Kenny whose mind was racing with a number of scenarios, none of which were particularly appealling.

"Ye know ah went tae Jamaica last May? Lovely place, first time ah've ever experienced an all inclusive holiday. Ye pay a big wedge up front bit after that fuck all, as yer food and bevvy is included. Went to this place called Sans Souci, without a care ah think it means, near Ocho Rios. The complete and utter dugs baws. On the second week ah went tae play a round o' golf and the steward at the club asks if ah would mind pairin up with this boy called Leo who was over fae Estonia. Leo was sufferin ah can tell you, couldnae handle the heat. Ah wasnae much better but ah had a hat on and had been stayin off the bevvy. He'd just done a big lunch wi wine and beer so was right oot the game. We get to the fourth hole and he fucken collapses. Ah thought it was a heart attack but it was just wee bit of sunstroke."

"Anyway, ah get him back to the clubhouse on the golf cart, ah was drivin like Jackie Stewart ah could tell ye. So he gets taken off to hospital but the next day comes roond the hotel looking brand new. He's brought me a bottle of champagne as a thank you and we get intae a wee bit of a chat. Turns oot he's in the same line as me"

"What, he makes tartan tat, Scotland souvenirs?" asked Kenny in an innocent tone. Harold's legitimate front was a souvenir company, run in the main by Alison, Kenny's wife.

"No, ya daft bastart. Crime wi a capital C. Ah never realised there was so much goin on in these old commy countries. So he's invited me over for a look see to see if we can work somethin oot the gither. This Scotland trip sounds like ideal cover so it's up tae you tae get me sorted. Ah think ah'd look good in a "c u Jimmy hat"?" Harold laughed but Kenny didn't join in. This was his worst nightmare come true, short of England winning the World Cup again, chaperoning Harold MacMillan on a Scotland trip won hands down. No way. No fucking way. How would he break this to Gus?

"Are you sure you're really going to need me, Harold? You're a well travelled man, what can I help you with?" Kenny realised a completely pathetic tone had crept into his voice but going anywhere with Harold had to be avoided at all costs.

"Ye know how tae make me look like a real fan. How am ah goin tae get tickets for the game? Ah want this to be as official as possible fur me and the boys."

"The boys are coming as well? Oh for fuck's sake" said Kenny. It was a blustery day outside but the shiver Kenny felt had nothing to do with the weather. He should have realised from the start Harold would not be flying solo to somewhere like Tallinn. The boys, as he casually referred to them were his minders. The sort of people that ate lightly poached lightbulbs for breakfast, washed down with a couple of mugs of brake fluid.

"Of course they are, ya thick bastart. Ahm no gaun over there withoot some back up. They'll be travellin as fans as well. Ah was thinking about buyin a kilt as well, to help blend in."

Fucking Mel Gibson, that Aussie bastard thought Kenny. He had noticed since the release of Braveheart the year before the number of guys wearing kilts had shot up. Gus witheringly referred to them as the "Braveheart boys" who now couldn't go to a game without painting half their face blue and wearing a kilt. He knew one boy from Canada, of all places, who'd gone the whole hog with the Braveheart gear and did look really good, but for the rest there was no hope. He'd seen a guy at Villa Park for the Holland game with just his eyes and the side of his forehead covered in blue facepaint. He hadn't been too pleased when Gus had told him "Never mind Braveheart son, you look like the Tartan Lone Ranger".

"I think a kilt might be a wee bit over the top, Harold just for a couple of games. Then again, you could wear it to weddings and other sorts of functions," said Kenny. "If you want tickets, you'll have to join the supporters travel club. I can organise that for you but I'll need three passport photos, one for each of you. I'll get the forms and we can take it from there. You're really sure about this?"

Kenny had visions of his father-in-law ending up in a gulag somewhere in Siberia and Alison nipping his head all the time about how he'd got her father into trouble. Got her father into trouble? Aye right.

"Sure? Sure ahm sure. It will be a wee family holiday, just me, you and the boys"

"But I normally travel with Gus," Kenny felt he had to make a stand somewhere and this was the easiest way of doing it.

"What? The poisoned dwarf will be there as well? Magic, he's always good value the wee man, tell him ah look forward to meetin up wi him again."

Kenny suddenly remembered Harold setting up Gus with a ladyboy on Kenny's stag trip in Amsterdam. They'd found a bar staffed entirely by gorgeous Thai transsexuals, then Harold had bribed one of them to do the business. Harold had warned Kenny but nobody told Gus. One of the boys organised a raffle for a blow job and had fixed it so Gus won. They had been sitting downstairs in the hotel bar when Gus returned from his winning assignation somewhat pale faced. He'd refused to tell them what had happened but Kenny had later prised it out of him.

"She was getting' into it good style man and ah got bit carried away. Put my hand up her skirt and got a bit more than ah expected like. Her baws was like two fuckin hard boiled eggs in a hanky, ahm tellin ye. Ah just shot ma load and got the fuck out of there. Did you know it was a bloke before ah went in?"

Kenny had lied, saying he thought it was a woman but he knew Gus still suspected him.

Kenny's thoughts drifted back to the present. "Ok, well that'll be 75 quid to sort out the membership of the supporters club," said Kenny trying to focus on what needed to be done.

"That's a bit pricey just for joinin a supporters club. Is it honestly 25 notes a head?" said Harold who was looking a bit stunned at the news of this expense.

Kenny stood up and had a big smile on his face "No, its only a tenner each membership but you owe me 45 quid for the fare here. You did say to put it on the meter"

* * * * *

Atholl lay back in his sofa and tried to collect his thoughts. He'd had a busy time at work setting up some bodyguards for UN officials in Rwanda. The feedback from the first few personnel he'd sent out had been so bad they'd had trouble getting new people. On top of that, there was his father's request that he kill a complete stranger who, apparently, was his half-brother. The detective agency had finally come up with the goods regarding Kenneth or Kenny, as he was known, Bradley. He'd read the file twice making notes as he went and felt he was finally getting an understanding of his quarry. He'd been inclined, yet again, to question the amount of detail but there was a covering letter from the agency saying they could do no more without attracting unwanted attention.

Atholl had noted that he travelled abroad a lot, both with his wife and on his own. Kenny appeared to be a keen follower of the Scotland football team but these trips he makes without the wife. He'd searched his memory for some image of a Scottish player or the national team but Atholl had spent his formative years outside Scotland at Eton and Oxford so had no great interest in the national teams of any sport. People expected him to be interested in rugby, given his background, and he had been down to Richmond to see London Scottish a couple of times but just didn't really feel comfortable. He'd always been a bit of a loner and the one area of his schooling he'd found difficult was forced participation in team sports.

As he read about Kenny's travels, Atholl formulated a plan. He'd heard of the trouble caused abroad by England fans and he could remember some match from the mid 80's when a large number of people had died in Rotterdam or Brussels or somewhere. Atholl had been up to his neck in death and brutality himself at the time so had paid it little heed. If he, Atholl, went abroad with lots of other fans, the chances of him getting noticed would be lessened. He couldn't go as a fan as he simply knew nothing about the game. What he needed was cover, a role to play but as whom? He tried to think of a reason why he would want to talk to people and appear genuinely interested. He could say he was on business but that would appear suspicious if he kept on turning up at games. Maybe a journalist? Yes, a freelance journalist, someone working on commission from a foreign magazine, trying to identify different types of football fans. He thought about changing his name but he had been working under the alias of Andy Muir since leaving the army so had no real problem over his identity. He didn't plan to make himself that well known. But back to the assignment, were all football fans animals? Why do they go abroad to drink and fight? He wondered when the next away game was. He would get his personal assistant to find out the next day.

He got up from the settee and wandered through his open french windows out on to the patio. It was a warm day and summer looked like it had finally appeared in London. The only trouble was it was the first week of August but better late than never he supposed. He paced up and down the patio for another couple of minutes and then realising he had just about managed to totally confuse himself he went back inside. He tried to create a plan of action in his mind but it was no good. He much preferred to sit down and write it out. He pulled an A4 pad out of a bureau drawer and took it over to the coffee table by the settee. He started sketching out his plan of operations.

If he went to an away game, he could try to meet up with the fans in the city. There couldn't be that many fans going to an away match could there? He could seek out Kenny Bradley in the crowd. Hopefully, having met him and established a rapport, Kenny's guard would be down and he could start and finish the job in double quick time. The job must be completed to both his and his father's satisfaction. Thinking about killing his half-brother had initially disturbed Atholl. He wondered if getting to know him would deter him from his task but he felt it could be achieved in a straightforward, single minded manner. He knew Kenny Bradley's life from the file and felt he wouldn't be missed. His wife might grieve for a bit but life goes on he thought and he, Atholl Forbes Lothian Farquharson McClackit, must become the sole claimant to the title, Clan Chief of the Clan McClackit.

As he pondered his destiny, Atholl realised he had better get his old kit out. He did laugh when he saw these American films where the assassin has every gadget under the sun. James Bond was a joke to most people who'd served in the forces but it never ceased to amaze him the American fixation with hardware. He preferred to travel light, knowing just how much havoc could be wreaked with a couple of simple tools and a creative imagination. Time to disturb the fishes he thought. In a corner of the lounge Atholl kept a reasonable sized fish tank. His friends had teased him about it, asking him when he was going to get his own private bar installed next to it like some Doncaster builder. Atholl had laughed but he'd never seen the humour in those private bars. He's seen quite a few in Loyalist households in Ulster where he'd received superb hospitality and knew that when you dare not go out of an evening for fear of being shot, they could be a big consolation. The fish tank served a couple of purposes for Atholl. It had surprised him what a turn on it had been for a number of women, especially the little beauty from Japan who thought he was keeping the fish as a source of food. She had even offered to make him some fresh seafood sushi with the contents of the tank. His main aim when buying the tank had been to provide cover for a couple of pieces of equipment he didn't really want lying about the house. One was a Smith and Wesson pistol he had removed from the hand of a dead terrorist in Northern Ireland. The other was his little box of tricks which he didn't think the police would appreciate a civilian being in the possession of.

He removed the lid of the tank and picked up a large rock from one of the corners. In the opposite corner a similar sized rock contained his pistol. Atholl lay the rock on a towel he'd put down on the carpet. Once he'd dried it off, he turned it so the base was facing him and unscrewed a couple of large plastic screws. The base came away to reveal a black rubber zipped case about the size of a small filofax. Atholl removed it and unzipped

47

the case to reveal, what had previously been, the tools of his trade. Now that he considered the contents, he wondered how he'd achieved so much with so little. He hadn't had the case out for a few months, the last time was to do a bit of maintenance on the equipment to keep it in good nick. He was struggling to remember the last time he'd used any of the gear in anger. Then it came back to him, the French family next door and that dog of theirs. A very noisy alsatian which would bark loudly for hours, day or night, at the slightest provocation. Atholl had always loved animals, especially dogs, but the last straw had come on the 13th of July the previous year. Having fully celebrated the glorious 12th of July with an old army colleague who shared his love of the Protestant cause, Atholl had been awoken from his alcohol induced slumber by the dog next door. His hangover had maintained its consistency for the rest of the day, in much the same way as the dog had continued to bark.

When the French family left for a Bastille day celebration at the French Embassy on the 14th, Atholl had decided enough was enough and the dog had to go. Looking back, he was shocked how much it had upset him when he had killed the dog by driving a whelk removing implement into the dog's ear. Well, at least the tool was French, he supposed, as he'd stolen it from a seafood restaurant in Saint Malo. He struggled to come to terms with his his unhappiness at first, especially when he'd done much worse to numerous members of the public in Northern Ireland. He'd knocked the dog out by throwing a fillet steak stuffed with three sleeping tablets to it over the fence separating the two courtyards. The beauty of the whelk tool was that it left minimal external damage whilst skewering the brain.

He looked down at it now, nestling between his rubber coated pliers, a tube of electrical jelly and the three industrial strength bangers. On the other side of the holder were his knife, some pipe cleaners, a military issue cigarette lighter and a small bottle of a clear liquid, the contents of which were both highly flammable and highly poisonous. Atholl tested each part of the kit where he could. Everything seemed in good working order, unaffected by the time spent in the fish tank. He zipped up the case and put it back in the hollow rock.

Screwing the base back on, he felt a small thrill at getting back to what he knew best, getting back in the saddle, so to speak. Thinking of that, didn't he have the number of that little Japanese filly somewhere? Sushi might not be on the menu but he definitely felt like something Japanese.

Chapter 4

Vienna

IT HAD BEEN an innocuous enough comment on what good shops there were at Heathrow these days, but it had been enough to set Gus off, "Economic apartheid, that's what this is, like. The haves versus the have nots, rich versus poor, the financially franchised against the economically disenfranchised. Are you listenin to me?"

Gus took a mouthful of lager and gave Kenny a pitying look. "Ah thought we were all part o' Europe now. One big happy EE fuckin C but no. Every time we want tae go tae somewhere in Europe, we're forced tae come through London, boost their bloody economy whilst deludin ourselves this is the golden age o' travel and we should be happy they're actually lettin us use this shitehole o' an airport to get out of the UK. We're just economic units to these people like, customers not passengers, mere units to be counted and discounted as the years progress. Bought and sold for English gold right enough."

Gus paused for another mouthful of Carling. "You can hardly find a seat, like, they've opened up so many shops. Why don't they close down fucken Harrods and put in a bar? Eh? That would keep the punters happy but here we aw are, crammed into some mock fucken olde English pub shoebox that looks like it was nicked from the original set of Emmerdale fucken Farm. Heathrow man, you can fucken keep it."

"So on your list of hatreds Gus, where would Heathrow come? Above or below Tenby?" asked Donny.

"Lower down than farmers?" asked Kenny.

"Aye don't worry, those rural bastards are still number one. Ah admit tae be being pretty much a son of the soil myself, coming from Dumfries, like, but ah've yet to see a poor farmer. And they all moan like fuck. The dairy ones are the worst, goin on about havin to work 365 days of the year because the cows won't milk themselves. Then goin on to say the farm has been in their family for four generations. Well hello, let's wake up and smell the Bovril, pal. If you grew up on a farm where you could see your old grandad and then your dad working 365 days of the year, did the penny not drop a career as a lion tamer even might be a little less demandin? Don't get me started." said Gus. His mouth opened again but this time for lager. A quick swallow later he continued.

"To go back to your original point on Heathrow's place in ma league o' hate it's probably equal with Tenby in terms of pure dislike. Slightly ahead on goal difference ah suppose as I have to pass through it so often. The funny thing is ah don't hate England or the English. Had many a good night in Blackpool like, then again maybe that's only because ah was wi a load of Scots but there's a good time to be had in London town by the way. Then again preferably when its not a Wembley weekend and every muppet and his brother from north of Gretna become Scotland fans. Last summer was alright but ye cannae win. No wanks from Scotland with their Bay City Roller gear on but loads of English casuals looking to kick fuck out of ye if you've got the slightest bit of tartan. Fuckin Gary McAllister. Right who wants another? Whats that cloudy stuff your drinking Kenny? It looks like somethin you'd find at the bottom of a barrel, for fucks sake."

"Its called Hoegaarden, it's a Belgian wheat beer and it's a magic drink. I'll have another pint. You should try it. What's Tenby ever done to you by the way?"

"A long story, best kept for another day" said Gus with a rather guilty look on his face.

There were five of them sitting in a transit lounge at Heathrow Terminal 2. Kenny and Gus had met Donny, another regular traveller on the flight down. A couple of new guys making their first trip were also in their company. They had flown down from Glasgow earlier that morning to get a connecting flight to Vienna for the Austria v Scotland game on the Saturday. Kenny had heard about this Belgian beer that was being released on to the UK market so thought he would give it a try. It had been tasty enough and he was feeling pleasantly mellow. Not normally a feeling he associated with a Scotland trip, but then again, they hadn't been to the game yet so no doubt a maelstrom of unpleasant emotions lay in store for him.

"Aye, maybe ah will. Always up for a new experience, alcohol wise," said Gus with a wide grin on his face.

"You going to buy this out of your winnings from yesterday?" asked Kenny with a big grin.

"Oh no, Gus," said Donny in a tone of surprise, "you've never been back on the gee gees. William Hill must be laughing all the way to the bank"

"Ha, fucken ha. Ah was a wee bit unlucky wi ma four selections like" snorted Gus.

Kenny exploded with laughter. "A wee bit unlucky? Three came last and one died".

The group burst out laughing leaving Gus picking his way through the chairs muttering, "Miserable cunts, the lot o' youse"

Gus headed off to the bar and Kenny turned to his mates, "Wait until he gets the price of the round off the barman. This stuff is £3.20 a pint"

"No way," said Donny. "There'll be a riot."

"No, the barman is safe but I'll get it big time. When he comes down here Gus likes to pretend he's the last of the big spenders and nothing fazes him. I reckon he'll have gone up the bar with a tenner, expecting it to cover five drinks and he's going to be donald ducked when he gets the final sum. Pity about the horses."

They all turned to look at the bar where Gus was speaking to another customer as he was waiting for the drinks to be poured. The barman put the last two pints of Hoegarden in front of Gus and entered all the prices on the till. He looked up and mouthed a figure at Gus. All they could see was the sight of Gus's shoulders tense involuntarily. He appeared to say something to the barman who repeated the figure. Another tense of the shoulders was cancelled by him reaching for his wallet in his sporran.

At this point, the other customer at the bar leant across and gave the barman a note, indicating for him to keep the change. Gus turned to face the other customer and said something. He then nodded in the direction of the rest of the party. They picked up the drinks between the two of them and came back to the group.

"Alright boys, this is Andy Muir but watch what ye say, he's a fucken journo. That's the down side. The good side is he's on expenses and has just got this round in. As for you Bradley, ya cunt. £3.20 for a pint of Belgian bottom of the barrel. You must be off yer heid. Ah telt ye Andy, he's a wind up bastart".

Andy sat down, trying not to look too concerned over Gus' introduction.

"This is extraordinarily fortunate for me. To meet you guys here is really excellent news. I've just been commissioned to write an article on the Scotland fans who support the the football team. Some might say you were a Tartan Army". These words were spoken in the rounded tones of a classically educated English actor. The guys were pretty taken aback by the accent but the last comment left them looking awkwardly at their feet.

"Eh, you could say that, Andy " said Kenny, "a tartan army indeed".

"Of course, I immediately feel part of it as I am Scottish myself."

"Aye right", said Gus "You can cut out the wind up now Andy. You sound more like Laurence Olivier than Kenny Dalglish."

"Well, be that as it may, I am a Glasgow man myself" said Andy, a confident smile beaming across his face.

Loud guffaws echoed round the company.

"A Glasgow man. Who's your team in Glasgow then?" asked Kenny, who was thinking we've got a right one here.

"I'm not really a follower of one team but if you push me, I am a bit of a Clyde fan" replied Andy.

This just gets better and better" said Kenny. "I can see you going down a storm at a Bully Wee social"

"I am sorry, "a Bully Wee social?"" asked Andy with a bewildered look on his face. The others looked at each other and decided the guy was either a care in the community case or having a wind up.

"It doesnae matter Andy. We'll fill you in on the details on the flight." said Gus, trying not to look too guilty for bringing a complete dickhead into the company. To cover his embarrassment, he proceeded to neck most of his Hoegaarden in one go.

"No a bad drop Kenny, even if it is a mortgage job for a round. Right, who wants another?" asked Gus.

"They've just called the flight Gus, I think we'd better get to the gate" said Donny.

"What's yer rush? Andy here'll see us alright for a round of halves, a wee freshener before the stewardess comes round wi the trolley. What d'ye say, Andy?

"Well, I…. "Andy had taken one sip from his pint of Guinness"

"Good man, come on and gie's a hand to carry the drinks back"

Gus had dragged Andy back up the bar whilst the rest of them started to get their bags together.

"What do you make of him then, Kenny?" asked Donny.

"I don't know but he's the poshest speaking Clyde fan I've ever met." replied Kenny.

They had all stood up by the time Gus and Andy returned from the bar. Gus had gone for a large gin and tonic but had bought, or rather got Andy to buy, vodka and cokes for the rest of them. These were duly despatched and they made their way to the flight.

By this stage, the three large Bloody Marys in Glasgow airport, the three pints of lager plus the Hoegaarden and a large gin and tonic were starting to have an effect on Gus. He was all over poor Andy like a rash, gibbering on about the kilt being the greatest aphrodisiac in the world, the women he'd shagged because of it, how everyone in the Tartan Army was equal and it was the only army in the world with no officers.

Kenny remembered Gus was normally a bit of a media tart, if any photographer turned up with a camera before a game, Gus would be girning away in front of the camera trying to get his photo in the paper. Sadly, the only time he'd made the front page was when he'd passed out on a car bonnet in Paris and his kilt had ridden up to show the tattoo of an octopus on his left buttock. A few people had started calling him Captain Nemo after that incident until Gus pointed out it wasn't in fact a tattoo of an octopus, it wasn't a tattoo at all but the remnants of a follow through when he thought he was about to fart and it had turned into something a bit more substantial.

As they were queueing to get on the plane, Kenny realised something wasn't right. A minor twitch in his bowel regions had grown into a spasm and he suddenly began to regret drinking the Hoegaarden. And to think he'd just been laughing at Gus' gut problems. He'd suffered from irritable bowel syndrome in the past, the only humorous side to it being when he told Gus who had proceeded to ask him, in all seriousness, if he planned to go and see a speech therapist. Kenny realised the cloudy effect in the Belgian beer may have been through added wheat. All of a sudden he became very concerned but then realised he should make it to the loos on board in plenty of time. He calmed down on realising this but as he relaxed, he let off a silent fart. Oops he thought and immediately looked around for someone to blame for the smell, so casting suspicion onto some other poor passenger. The first person to his left was Andy. There's something no right about you pal, he thought, so you might as well cop for this one.

"Jeezo, was that you Andy? That's minging." Kenny pulled a face which didn't take too much effort as it was a totally gross fart combining an essence of the yeast of the Hoegaarden, the beans from cooked breakfast he'd had at Glasgow airport and a touch of the Guinness he'd been drinking last night.

"Holy fuck, Andy" cried Gus. "There's women and children present here for fucks sake, that could stunt the wee yins growth"

Andy looked bemused at this until the smell hit him full on up both nostrils. "Dear God! What is that smell?"

"Calm down Andy" said Gus "Ah think ye've attracted enough attention to yirsel by other means, like. Don't want to over egg the pudding old boy as you've clearly over egged something already judging by that fart ye've just dropped"

"You don't think that was me, do you?" Andy looked around him to be met by reproachful stares by a number of passengers plus a steward who'd been alerted to the smell by another passenger.

As they approached the door the steward looked down at Andy and asked if everything was alright.

"Yes, fine thank you" was the reply.

"Well, if you are in need of any assistance sir, we are always on hand to help but I hope you can appreciate how awkward it can be for other travellers if passengers have difficulty controlling themselves." commented the steward.

"You tell him pal, that was Charles Laughton so it was, like. Andy, if you're going hang around wi us pal, no more of the human stink bombs, the only person ah know that does it worse than you is that bastart, Bradley. Hey, wait a minute, Kenny, have you just papped the blame onto Andy here?

Gus was trying to progress down the aisle while shouting at Kenny, "It's not on big man, it's just not on."

Andy struggled into his window seat and sat down. Kenny had gone too far down the plane and on his return arrived at the correct row at the same time as Gus.

"Don't worry Kenny, ah'll just sit next to Andy to give him the lowdown on the TA. He'll get no decent info from a borin bastart like you."

"That is actually my seat," replied Kenny in a somewhat pissed off tone, as Gus sat down next to Andy in the middle seat.

"Ah know, but it's only a wee flight, we'll be there in no time. You just take mine on the aisle while ah talk to Andy." Gus had a pleading look on his face as he was saying this, barely masking his desperation to get his name in the magazine.

"Ok, have it your way." said Kenny and sat down in the aisle seat.

As soon as they took off, Gus passed out and slumped on Atholl's shoulder. This was not the way things were meant to turn out thought Atholl. An old contact from way back had been looked up. This chap was a senior manager with BA who had worked with Atholl in Northern Ireland. Atholl had taken an educated guess the lack of direct flights between Glasgow and Vienna would force Kenny Bradley to fly via London with BA. His friend Rufus had run a couple of checks and been able to provide all the necessary details to Atholl. When he arrived, he had told the girl at the check-in desk he was meeting a friend airside so could he please sit next to him on the flight. He had tried to talk over or rather through Gus' head to Kenny but had been getting little or no joy. His target seemed reluctant to engage in conversation and Atholl realised that in attempting to talk about football, he was only digging a bigger hole for himself.

By this time Kenny had had enough. Like a lot of football fans he was barely tolerant of people who had no idea about the game but felt they could talk endless pish on the subject. Most of them betrayed a lack of knowledge of the game but also, and more importantly to Kenny, a lack of feeling for the game. The way things were going, Andy was going to get a gold medal for knowing nothing about football. The beautiful game? He wouldn't know a football if it bounced off his head. Kenny's antennae were twitching after Andy's question about the Bully Wee, which any self respecting football fan knew was the nickname of Clyde.

As the aeroplane had taken off, Andy had asked him if he thought Scotland would win. Kenny had replied they could well get a result as they had won the friendly the last time they played in Vienna. Andy had then made the cardinal error of asking who they'd played in the friendly. Kenny had initially thought he was taking the piss then realised it was a serious question.

"They beat Austria 2-1." was his reply

"Oh, it was Austria they were playing was it?" asked Andy,

aware that he'd said something wrong but not quite sure what it was.

"Aye, who else would Scotland be playing in Vienna?" came the reply from Kenny in a tone of voice Andy felt bordered on the hostile.

That clinched it for Kenny. This prick didn't even realise Scotland would be playing Austria in Austria. Kenny needed a drink. Fortunately, the stewardess was just approaching with the drinks trolley. He ordered a large Bloody Mary and tried to relax. In doing so, he ignored Andy's efforts at restarting the conversation by asking where they planned to go out tonight.

Gus and Kenny had heard of an area called the Bermuda Triangle which was the nightlife centre of Vienna. That was where they were headed but hopefully it would be a journo free zone, thought Kenny. Then again, if Andy was still on expenses, Gus would be sticking to him like glue. Gus and free drink? It didn't bear thinking about.

Another issue was the U21 game tomorrow. Where the fuck was Amsteten? It sounded like a nice wee day trip out of Vienna, have a few beers, mix with the locals and hopefully get a result before heading back into Vienna for a good night out. The bulk of the travelling support would be arriving on the Friday so there would be a big crowd of Scots out on the town at night.

Just as Kenny started to think who else would be travelling, Gus woke up. He attempted to straighten up and stretch in the limited space of his seat but his neck had cramped up, as his head had been lying at an angle of ninety degrees when he passed out on Andy.

"Ooh, ya bastard," he cried out as he attempted to move his

head. "Christ, could ye no have done somethin for me, Andy? Neck's fucken killin' me, like. Might have to get it massaged when we get to Vienna or maybe even get one o these stewardesses to do the necessary. Might even get asked if ah want extras, eh?"

He turned to Kenny with a grinning leer on his face, "What's wrong wi your greetin face Bradley? Did ye no get me a drink when the burd came round with the trolley? It's all about you ya bastard. Ye don't think of your travellin buddies in the slightest. It's all me, me, me with you pal."

"I thought you'd had enough, given the Sleeping Beauty act" said Kenny, "Andy's worried you were ignoring him".

"That right, Andy? It was the early morning call that did for me then. Some guys get a hard on when a plane takes off, I just fall asleep. Never been able to work out why, like"

"Nothing to do with the copious amounts of alcohol you consume before you set foot on a flight?" asked Kenny.

"Ah, shut it, you. Ye ken, ahm a nervous flyer and the drink's jist to calm my nerves. Anyway Andy, ah'll no be ignorin you the night. You're wi us an we're goin to show you a night in Vienna ye'll never forget."

"Really, can't wait" said Andy in a less than enthusiastic tone.

"Me neither" said Kenny in an equally subdued tone. He realised this was going to be a night to remember, probably for all the wrong reasons, if Andy was coming along.

Chapter 5

Tadger's Last Stand

TADGER CURRIE SAT at the back of Molly O'Driscoll's, Vienna's finest Irish bar, nursing the last of his lager and lime. The pub sound system was playing a song that seemed to be called "Macarena". He thought it must be some kind of advert but every time it came on these burds started doing a weird dance. He wasn't happy to be drinking this lager and lime pish but this was one of the occasional pitfalls of minesweeping for drinks. "What sad prick drinks this stuff," he thought to himself before realising he was that sad prick. Ok then, what sad prick pays money to drink this pish was a thought that went down better than the lager and lime.

He'd picked it up from a table near the gents so had marked the area off in his mental quadrant. He'd once seen a TV programme where it showed the police at a crime scene marking off the area in squares. He thought he would apply that to his minesweeping technique. It had paid off brilliantly, apart from a couple of times when the drink had caused him to forget he'd already passed one square of the grid and the drinkers were only too aware of what he was up to. He was sure he'd had a mouthful of piss in that Mexican bar in Moscow last year but again, it was a small price to pay when the commie bastards were charging a fiver a pint for lager, well, ex commie bastards, he supposed.

The lime had left a bad taste in his mouth and he needed something to cleanse his palate. The bar had warmed up nicely, as he knew it would. Scotland fans and Irish pubs were made for one another when you travelled abroad. A large number of fans only drank dark beer at home and were prepared to pay for Guinness rather than drink lager all the time on foreign trips. A white wine spritzer would be nice but then he remembered Austrian wine making was famed for its liberal use of anti freeze in its winemaking process. Fuck that, he thought I want to cleanse my palate no strip it bare.

He was about to head off to a new square on the grid when he saw a couple of faces enter the bar that were as welcome to Tadger as a kick in the puss. Kenny bloody Bradley and the wee nyaff Gus McSween. They'd sussed him a long time ago for his drink hoovering antics and he owed them. In fact, thinking back, they were standing very close to that table in Moscow last year when he'd picked up the glass of lager or rather what he thought was lager. It wasn't beyond that McSween to pull that sort of stunt.

Then there was that round they'd conned him into buying in Sweden last year. Told him the wee sister of one of the burds they were with was right into him and it would greatly help his cause if he bought a drink for her. He's gone up to get one in for the lassie as it was a good deal. She'd only wanted a Sprite, but then she came up to the bar and said she didn't have any money so could he possibly get a drink for her sister and their two friends? Apparently, they had been very good to her by taking her out for a meal the night before. Put him right on the spot it did but he's seen the bigger picture and knew the possibilities of what lay ahead wi this hot Scandinavian babe, especially as he liked them young.

25 quid for four fucking drinks never mind the Sprite. Bradley and McSween both had nips with a bottle of coke as a mixer for each of them and the burds were drinking wine. Seven pound each for a glass of wine a fly couldnae do a breast stroke in! The final insult came when he asked the wee lassie why she wasnae drinking. She said she had to leave soon to get home to do her homework. Homework indeed! The very mention of the word made him remember how they'd stitched him up. Not only that, they'd then left to go to a nightclub with the burds having drunk their round and bought him fuck all. As he thought of this, Tadger got more and more angry, thinking payback time is here for Tadger Currie and its Messrs Bradley and McSween that will be footing the bill. He could make out a third person with them who was just going up to the bar. Another wee guy but his face wasn't familiar. Ah well, it looked like he was getting the round in so it would only be a matter of time before it was a target rich environment.

Atholl struggled to the bar. He was sweating heavily but that was more to do with the crush than what he was about to attempt. He had tried to remain cool and collected but McSween had got on his nerves to such an extent he thought he might as well try and remove him from the picture. Not permanently, as with Bradley, but just teach him a lesson, a couple of nights in hospital, say, ensuring he would miss the match. Fortunately, they'd both asked for vodka and lemonades so it wouldn't take much poison to do the job. They'd both headed off to the gents so he made his way to a column with a little shelf, allowing Atholl to easily hide the drinks from view. People were too busy having a good time to pay much attention to what he was doing and Atholl realised he was having a good time himself. Back in the old routine or what? The larger dose of the drug was swiftly poured into Bradley's drink and a second, much smaller amount, went into McSween's. Andy had never used this stuff before on a job but it came highly recommended from one of his company's employees who swore by the stuff for an effective, but clean removal of an enemy. There was a slight aftertaste but by the time the drinker had realised, they were halfway dead.

He was awaiting their return when he realised someone was standing next to him, staring across the bar. The somewhat miserable looking man then motioned to him with his head. As Andy moved towards him the man said to him "Ye're in there, pal"

"What?"

"Ah said, ye're in there pal, rat blonde in ra corner"

"What are you talking about?"

"Rat blonde is hotter ran the Sahara for ye pal. Jist hae a look"

Atholl realised what the man meant and turned round to look at the blonde but it was like a Hitler youth rally in the pub. How many blonde Austrians could you expect in a Viennese bar? He looked in vain for a blonde who was giving him the eye but the only person giving him the eye was McSween, beckoning him to come over with the drinks.

"I don't think she's looking at me" he said and turned to an empty space. The guy had vanished.

Better get to the others thought Andy and reached for the vodka and lemonades. They were gone, a couple of wet glass stains on the shelf were all that remained of his poisoned chalices.

Oh shit, thought Atholl. Somebody's nicked the drinks. He looked around to see if anyone had clearly picked up a vodka and lemonade by mistake but it was all sweaty beer stained guys in kilts holding pints of lager or Guinness. A couple gave him a funny look when they found him staring at their drinks but he was too worried about other matters to let that concern him. He felt an urgent tugging at his sleeve and turned round to see McSween's contorted face looking at him.

"Did ye get a round in?"

"Yes, but"

"Yes but what, Andy? You've been away so long, ah thought you were distillin the vodka, where's the drinks?"

"They've been taken, there's been a terrible mistake"

"Whit? The only mistake you've made is takin yer eye off the ball man. Ye should know what these cunts are like if anybody leaves a drink unattended. Come on, lets get back tae the bar. We've got three real honeys lined up over there, like. As ah said before, the kilt is the greatest aphrodisiac known to man. Ye'll be knocking them dead in five minutes, Andy"

Tadger Currie stood close to the entrance of the bar, ready for a quick getaway should he be spotted. He didn't plan to savour the drinks as he would need to polish them off quickly and find another bar. The first one tasted a bit off when it went down, must be using cheap vodka, the tight bastards, he thought. He thought about cutting his losses and leaving the other but then thought, fuck it and necked the second in a oner. Rough as fuck man, wait a minute, really rough.............

66

Kenny was thinking times just get better and better. He was in deep with a gorgeous Austrian who reminded him of Michelle Pfeiffer, always a bit of a fave. Her brother was on the door, so it was also looking good for a lock-in, should they not already be installed in the hotel before closing. Might need to have a word with the wee man to ensure that if he pulled, he was going back to the burds as opposed to the hotel. He was wondering how to break it to the wee man when Else came back from the ladies

"You crazy Scots guys drink too much, you know?"

"Aye well, if you'd grown up in Dumfries in the 1970's you might have a drink problem. Has some cun, er has somebody been hassling you?"

"No, my brother has to lie a guy on a table. He has fallen, He is helpless."

"He'll be alright, must have been drinking some of that wine of yours with the anti-freeze in it."

All of a sudden Kenny felt a chill in the air. "That is not funny, you know. Many wine producers add chemicals to help the wine mature".

"Aye, fair enough but anti freeze?"

"Well nobody asks you to drink it, you know" she replied

"Speaking of drinks can I get you another?"

"No, I have a headache and I think I must now go home" was the cool reply. Else picked up her bag and walked towards the exit. Kenny finished his beer and stared at the empty glass in his hand.

Kenny was pissed off but determined not to show it. "Ok then, catch you later" he murmured. Pissed off right enough but not with the Austrian girl, with himself. How many times had he got into a good position with a foreign lassie then blown it?

Just at that moment Gus bounced up with a large smile on his face.

"Ahm looking favourite for a leg over tonight, old boy. Want to make it a foursome?"

"No, I'm just going to stay here and catch up with a few guys" said Kenny.

"Ha ha, don't tell me bigmouth strikes again, you sad cunt. What did ye say to her? Ye'll be getting banned fae farms again wi that foot in mouth disease."

"We agreed to disagree on the benefits to Austrian wine of adding anti freeze to the end product."

"Adding anti-freeze to wine? Ye'd have been better off pourin it down the front o' her knickers. Right, well ah cannae carry any passengers as there's shaggin to be done, like. Don't wait up, big boy, see you in the mornin."

Kenny wondered what the fuck he was doing with his life at that particular moment in time. Scotland had better get a result tomorrow night or that was it with the Tartan Army. It had been a dark, dark night coming out of Villa Park after the Switzerland game earlier on that year and he didn't know how much more he could take. Hopefully this game would get them on track for France '98. Just when he thought things couldn't get any worse Andy appeared. Oh Christ, thought Kenny, Gus doesn't want to carry any passengers but I've got to put up with this prick.

"Where have you been?" asked Kenny. "I thought you were with some Austrian burd?"

"I was, but made a total mess of chatting her up. Probably asking if all Austrians really wanted to be Germans wasn't the smartest of moves and she's gone. What about you?"

"A similar fucking story. Maybe we've got more in common than I thought. " Kenny replied.

"I dare say," said Andy who had a slightly bemused smile on his face.

An almighty scream pierced the bar. Kenny looked over to the door to see a bouncer with his arms wrapped round a young blonde who was clearly having some kind of panic attack. A space had been cleared round a table where a body lay comatose. Kenny thought the figure looked vaguely familiar and then realised it was Tadger Currie.

"What the fuck has he gone and done now?" said Kenny to no one in particular.

"Do you know him?" asked Andy

"Know him? Suffered him more like. Tadger Currie the sweatiest boil on the sweatiest arse of the Tartan Army. A complete loser who comes on trips, mooches off other fans who don't know him and when you're back's turned, he'll hoover up all your bevvy. Gus got him a good one last year in Moscow when he got an empty pint glass and pee'd in it till it looked like half a pint of flat lager. Better go and see what's up with him."

"Well, if you know him on you go. I'll wait here".

"Suit yourself" said Kenny.

Atholl thought the body on the table may have been the guy who had distracted him earlier on and taken the drinks. From what Kenny had just said it seemed highly likely. Better not hang around the scene of crime he thought and headed off to the side exit. He consoled himself with the thought there would be plenty more opportunities and that he was just getting his eye in. Opportunities were all over the shop in this scrum of humanity.

As he approached the table, Kenny could see that the mood

had changed. The woman had been led away and two bouncers plus a guy Kenny presumed was the manager, judging by his suit and tie, stood by the table.

"Is he ok?" asked Kenny

"Nein" said the manager. "He is, how you say in English, dead as a doodoo".

"Dead drunk, I think you mean?"

"Kaput," said one of the bouncers who looked like he'd just found out steroids made you impotent.

"But how?" asked Kenny.

The manager said something in German and in response to Kenny's quizical look, one of the bouncers motioned with his cupped hand approaching his lips.

"Bevvy? No way. That prick would only expire through drink if he had to buy a round." Kenny looked round for Gus for some moral support but then remembered he was off on manoeuvres. He wondered if Andy would have any idea what to do but he had vanished.

"Fuckin' brilliant, last man standing again."

"What's goin on, Kenny?" said a voice behind him.

"Alright, Wullie." The man asking the questions was Wullie Fraser, a long time fellow traveller in the Tartan Army. "These guys seem think to think Tadger Currie's pegged it. I think he's just passed out wi the drink but I don't speak German and their English is about as good as mine. Any ideas?"

"Wait a minute, one of our lads was in the works in Munich. If I can get him away from this blonde, I'll see if he can get a translation going."

"I wouldnae rush if I was you Wullie. I think they might just have a point, the Austrian boys. Look at that"

Tadger's sporran had fallen to the side when they had laid him on the table. Initially Kenny had returned it to its proper place but it had moved once more. This had nothing to do with the movement of the crowd around him or the table but the fact that Tadger had a tent pole of a hard on. Where the sporran had previously been, it was once more dislodged and now replaced by a tartan teepee.

"Fuck me", said Wullie "it's Tadger's last stand."

Chapter 6

Back Home

THE FLIGHT BACK to Glasgow from Heathrow was relatively smooth. They'd only had a 30 minute wait between planes but it had still been enough to prompt a rant from Gus regarding the cheapness of duty free vodka at Heathrow compared to Glasgow airport. Kenny couldn't see the difference but didn't want to provoke a full scale outburst from the wee man so bit his tongue.

They'd spent the Sunday wandering round Vienna and Kenny had even managed to get Gus and a couple of others out to the Schonbrunn Palace outside the city where they had visited the Gloriette, which Kenny believed was a tribute to Empress Marie Theresien. This had provoked the comment from Gus that she must have been some ride if the boy saw fit to build something that big as a tribute to her. The only tribute he'd given to any of his conquests was to moo like a cow when he came but only if she was somebody really special.

Kenny had thought it best to keep them out of bars after Gus had earlier embarrassed everybody by finishing an Austrian bloke's lunch in an Irish bar. The guy had entered Molly Malone's and ordered haddock and chips plus a pint of Guinness. He'd drunk his pint but had taken only one bite of his fish and hardly any chips. All this had been keenly observed by Gus who had been appalled earlier at the prices charged for food and drink. The Austrian was barely out the door before Gus had swooped on his plate. His only comment was "Well, if he's no wantin it".

The game had been a pretty dull 0-0 draw but it was a reasonable start to the campaign as they would have settled for any kind of positive result pre match. Compared to the U21s the day before it was a real achievement. They'd gone down 4-0 in a match best described as a gubbing going on complete annihilation.

The three of them sat in a row on the shuttle to Glasgow. Donny, Kenny and Gus. They had received some funny looks from the air crew as they got on, given that Gus was still wearing his kilt and flip flops with a pair of white running socks. Any fears about getting removed from the flight had evaporated when a stewardess with a broad Glasgow accent had come up to them and asked them if they were getting back from Vienna.

When they said they were she replied, "No a bad point but we'll need tae dae better in the double header comin up. You'll be going to that ah take it."

When they nodded that they were, she continued "Well, youse had better get ready for aw that fanny in Tallinn. Ah wiz there fur a hen weekend last month. Talk aboot takin sandwiches tae a banquet, we felt right stupit cows. Nane o us got a lumber the whole weekend. Ah well, ah'll be round wi the drinks trolley in a few minutes so just let me know what youse are wantin."

"Aye, ye can take the girl out of Glasgow......" said Donny.

"Still cannae get over that gents man" said Gus. "That one with the self cleanin seat, like. The nummer of places ah've had a shite in that could do wi somethin like that doesnae bear thinkin about."

"Another thing that doesn't bear thinking about is the state of you after smokin one joint. What the fuck possessed you to try it again? You know what it does to you," said Kenny.

"Aye, it's a fair cop guv. Ah can only hold ma hands up and accept full responsibility for ma actions, like".

"More like inactions" piped up Donny "you were comatose outside the ticket gate. If Kenny hadnae come out to get you at half time you could have been lifted."

"Aye, ok, don't go on. Ah was a complete mess and ah know it. Must have been strong stuff, by the way, to leave me in that state, like."

"Fuck off. "Strong stuff"!!!! You eat a poppy seed muffin and you're in la la land. A Lemsip gives you hallucinations."

"Ok, ok, ah admit ahm a wee bitty susceptible to foreign substances and ah admit ah was in the wrong. Can we just file it under f for forget all the fuck about it," pleaded Gus.

"End my drug hell cries Angus McSween, 34 of Anniesland. I am addicted to Lemsips, Beechams Cold remedies, Tennents lager and the Scotland football team. His mercy cry echoes round Great Western Road as he struggles from day to day desparate for an Anadin extra or news of the latest Scotland squad"

"Aye awright, everone's a fucken comedian," muttered Gus

"You lads awright for drinks?" asked the cheery air stewardess.

"This your first day?" asked Donny

"No, why di ye ask?" she replied

"You seem remarkably cheery for an air hostess. I thought they'd have ground it out of you by now" said a very perplexed Donny.

"Maybe ahm just like you three"

Gus snorted derisively "How are you like us three?" he asked.

"Just naturally high on life, ya mug. Enjoy the rest of your flight". At this she turned and walked towards the rear of the plane.

"Ah could be in love" said Gus as he screwed his head round to get one last glimpse of the stewardess. "ah wonder if that English boy on the flight fae Vienna to London has worked out what ye were talkin about, Kenny.

"Fuck him" came the reply. "I know you don't have to be an arsehole to be English but in his case it definitely helped. What a prick. Speaking to strangers on planes is always dangerous but all I'll say is, he started it."

"What are you on about? " asked Donny.

"It must have been when you nodded off. This guy was a Geordie who loved jazz and just couldn't shut up about some Vienna jazz festival that was on at the weekend. When I told him I thought it was a lot of tuneless nonsense, he told me I just didn't understand the pain of jazz. I told him I perfectly understood the pain of jazz as my ears bled everytime I had to listen to that Coltrane pish. At that time I hadn't realised he was wearing two tone shoes, obviously from when he was stompin at the Savoy but his bowtie, braces and armbands should have alerted me to the fact he was an old jazzer. To appease him I said "Wasn't there a jazz blues film set in the north east?"

"Yes" he said

"Tommy Lee Jones played a villain"

"Yes" he replied.

"It was directed by Mike Figgis?"

"Yes"

"Sting was in it along with that blonde American actress Melanie Griffiths"

"Yes" he enthused, "have you ever seen it

"No" I said.

He gave me this queer look then gave up on me. He'd pissed me right off when he asked me not to crush his trilby in the over head locker when we got on. Fuck knows the state of that as I made sure my duty free landed right on it. More of a flat cap than a trilby now, I think."

The pilot's voice came over the aircraft speakers asking them to fasten their seatbelts and that it would be ten minutes to landing.

"Whatever happened about Tadger Currie?" asked Donny.

"I don't know. I saw a bloke's Daily Record at Heathrow and there was a few lines at the bottom of page 10 about his death. Just the usual, mystery of Scots fan's death in Vienna, blah, blah, blah."

"More than the miserable bastard ever deserved," said Gus

"How can you be so callous about the death of another human being?" asked Donny in mocking tones.

"Agh, shut it you. Folk are dying everywhere every second of every day, like. Tadger Currie wouldn't have pissed on any o us if we'd been on fire so no loss to me."

"Did it say anything about a cause of death?" asked Donny

"Suspected heart attack with an added complication of wallet failure. Nah, the heart attack was the most likely. It was lucky I didn't get roped into staying to identify the body. I gave the cops a complete statement as did Wullie so they accepted that. I think they were just relieved it wasn't related to any aggro" said Kenny.

Gus looked lost in thought but Kenny didn't think this was out of respect for Tadger.

Gus looked up, "Ah've just remembered, what happened to that journo called Andy?"

"I don't know" said Kenny "He vanished from that bar where Tadger died like snow off a dyke. Speaking of dyke's, Gus, how did you get on last night with that burd that looked like a lesbian?"

Gus thought back to last night and a resigned look passed across his face.

"Aye, it was a bad call by McSween on that one ahm afraid. Nice enough lassie, like, but neither me nor the rest of the male population of the western world was going to get anywhere wi her. Pity about that boy Andy. I thought he might have been on the same flight back as us. Could have ponced more drink off him at Vienna airport"

"Ah the new Tadger Currie is born" said Donny.

"Hey, less of that you cheeky bastard. Ah stand my round and you know that. Anyway Bradley, is there any money left in the kitty?"

"You mean, is there any money left after you did your best to spend it all on roses last night cause you thought the bird selling them wanted to get into your pants, as opposed to just getting into our kitty?" asked Kenny.

"That girl was gaggin for it man. Ye think ah was just buyin those roses to get her interested but you didnae see ma master scheme at work, if ah didnae get lucky wi her there's always have a plan B."

Kenny sighed heavily, "And this scheme was what? Buy loads of roses and if the seller gives you the bum's rush, you can then find another burd to try and woo her with all the flowers."

"Fuck's sake, was it that obvious? Ah must be losin my touch if a torn faced bastard like you can see the game plan and where it's leadin."

"It was going nowhere. How pished were you to buy all those roses when you know you get hayfever eating a salad! You must have sneezed twenty times in five minutes after she thrust that bunch in your face. She'll wearin a surgical mask the next time she goes out sellin after all the germs you sprayed in her face. Now that I think of it, you don't think that would help you with women?"

Gus looked up, "What ,buyin them roses?"

"No, you wearing a surgical mask. It would hide half your face which could only be a good thing," said Kenny

"Aye but what half would he wear it on though? The top or the bottom?" chipped in Donny.

"Ha fucking ha. The day ah need to take advice from the likes o' you with regard to the fairer sex is the day ah take a vow of celibacy, like. Right, where we going fur a drink when we land then?"

Kenny suddenly remembered he had agreed to meet Cammy in the Horseshoe at 6.30 that evening. The relationship between Cammy and Gus was one which had not taken off quite as well as Kenny had hoped. Gus's extreme homophobia couldn't see past the fact that, apart from being gay, he and Cammy had the same interest. Drinking, football and having as much gratuitous sex as possible. Gus was always polite in his company but Kenny knew he had a real issue with Cammy's homosexuality but there was nothing he could do about it.

"I'm meeting Cammy at 6.30 in the Horseshoe if you fancy it," murmured Kenny.

"Fan fucking tastic" replied Gus. "How is Govan's answer to Quentin Crisp these days? Has he moved to Queen's Park yet? That must be nap to be his spiritual home, like."

"Look, he likes you. I don't know why you have to be so antagonistic towards him."

"Thats jist the problem ya tube. Ah don't want him to like me, ah want him to fucken hate me, like. Wan step up from likin is fancyin and there is no way he's gettin anywhere near my arse, no wi ma piles, that's for certain"

"I honestly don't think you have anything to worry about on that score, he likes them young and slim, no middle aged wi a bum like a deflating airship. Come on let's get off this plane and get a bus into town."

As they entered the Horseshoe there was a muted air about the place. Only a few hardy soles had come out on the Monday night and others seemed intent on putting off the journey home for as long as possible. They walked round the bar till they found Cammy sitting at a table at the back. He was reading the report of the game in that night's "Evening Times".

As they approached he looked up and finished the last of his lager.

"As ever, Gus, perfect timing. I'll have a pint of Tennents my good man and if its service with a smile, you even get a wee tip." Cammy had long been aware of Gus's dislike for him and took sincere pleasure out of winding him up.

"For fuck's sake, ah've jist walked into the pub and ahm being financially raped. Still better than being raped in another way by the likes o you. Ok, what do you two want?

Gus got the order and headed off to the bar.

"Alright, Cammy, how's it going?" said Donny.

"No too bad, no too bad at all." He pointed to the paper, "Broon keeps this up, ah might have to look in my little black book for my contacts at PSG for France '98. Shite game but a good result from what I can make out. Watched it on the telly and nearly fell asleep it was so crap. A good trip nonetheless, I take it?"

"Aye, it was ok. Vienna's no the most mental of places but hopefully the next two venues will liven things up a bit.

"Oh aye," said Cammy, "Riga and Tallinn, the wild east. A good time should be had by one and all"

"You up for it, Cammy?" asked Donny.

"I'm always up for it Donny," said Cammy with a wicked leer, "you should know that. No, I'll be giving these two a miss as I am somewhat financially challenged at this moment in time. Anyway, speaking of being up for it, here's somebody who always raises something in me"

Gus had returned to the table with the pints and had just missed Cammy's last remark. He was looking in a happier state than when he'd left.

"What's wrong wi' you?" asked Kenny. "You look like your coupon's just come up"

"Might well have done, ye remember that burd ah had the interview wi about ma finances? Ah jist bumped into her at the bar. Gave her a bit o' chat and ahm jist heading back up there, like. Her tongue's got unfinished business wi ma cock."

"Aw Gus, leaving so soon? I was hoping we might get a chance to know each other a little better," said Cammy a disappointed pout on his lips. "You know my tongue is available for you any time, whatever business you may wish to complete."

"Aye well, when ah decide to go that way, they can dig me up and ye can open ma coffin for first dibs Cammy. This lassie could be the one, ye ken"

"Good luck but I thought you said she had the sexual prowess of a panda?" said Kenny " Oh well, I hope everything works out for you and its the real deal for a nuclear family McSween"

"Thanks very much Kenny, ah didnae see you being so positive aboot me and ma love life, like."

Cammy burst out laughing, "Gus, you don't see the bigger picture my wee tartan love terrorist. If you get married and settled down, Kenny here doesnae have the burden of you trailing round Europe with him. Talkabout a win win situation.´

At this last comment Gus turned and walked off muttering as he passed the drinkers at the bar.

Kenny turned to Cammy. "Speaking of family matters, how's your sister getting on Cammy?"

"Don't ask Kenny, it's a living nightmare" came the reply. "When Hughie finds out he'll kill the guy first and God knows what he'll do to my sister."

"Have I missed something?" said Donny

"Put it like this" said Cammy, "This live football will be the death of someone, namely the stupid wee tim who is shagging my sister."

"I still don't get it" said Donny.

"Ok, I'll paint you picture. A guy comes round to my sister's house to put in cable TV. Within twenty minutes its mad passionate how's your father on the kitchen table like Jack Nicholson and Jessica Lange in "The Postman Always Rings Twice". The only problem is he has the names of all the Lisbon Lions tattooed down his right arm. I'll never eat another meal at that table without thinking about Jinky Johnstone, I can tell ye, the amount of twisting and turning that must have gone on between that pair."

"Oh dear" said Donny.

"Oh dear, oh dear, oh dear says I when I find out. This is my own flesh and blood married to one of my closest mates and she's shagging a Celtic fan!"

"But what's all this got to do with live football on the telly?" said Donny.

"Well, before live football" said Cammy "you could set your watch by when a game would be played. Saturday afternoon at 3pm, one game at home one week and the following week an away match. Now wi' all this live pish screwing up the football calendar ma sister don't know when a shagging slot is going to become available. She's getting more and more worked up cos she's no getting her legover regular like. To make matters worse, Hughie is getting a wee bit suspicious of the phone ringing and nobody answering it when he picks it up."

"So is Hughie no doing the necessary between the sheets?" asked Kenny.

"Well, he says he is but I'm no sure. Ma sister says he's having a bit of a problem down below and it's the last straw as far she's concerned. This Celtic casanova has pushed her to the brink and she's even talking about leaving Hughie. I don't know how many services that engineer boy provides but he's definitely been laying more than cables. She cannae stop talkin' about him. Ahm usually right up for someone telling me about their sexual experiences with a man but only when it's a man telling me. It's disgusting some of the stuff you heteros get up tae". Cammy tried to take away the distaste of his sister on the job by swallowing a large mouthful of lager. The bar had filled up quite considerably for some reason and the trio fell silent as they considered Cammy's predicament.

"It's no an easy one and that's for sure" said Kenny trying to buy some time while thinking how to get out of the conversation and back home to Alison.

"Don't you worry about it, Kenny. I'll sort something out with the pair o' them," said Cammy "though what pair I don't know. Maybe I'll send Hughie on a TA trip wi Gus and he can fall for some sexy foreign babe to take his mind off things. Then again if he can't get it up, he's no use to no cunt. Literally."

* * * * *

Atholl sat back in his chair and pondered his next move. The light was fading in his lounge and he got up to switch on a lamp. The light illuminated a portrait his father had given him of Castle McClackit. It has actually been painted by Atholl's mother who, like Atholl, had maintained a profound dislike for the place all her life. It made him wonder if what he was doing was really necessary. Was it that important that he become the next chief of the McClackits? Living in the castle had driven his mother to suicide, well that and his father's continual cheating. Could he really risk everything he had built up just to lay sole claim to that hideous castle? He'd called home on his return to speak to his father. Potter had answered the phone and informed him the chief was entertaining at this moment in time and he could not be interrupted. Atholl took that as a good sign, as there was clearly a lot of life left in the old fellow yet.

Despite his failure to eliminate Kenny Bradley in Vienna, Atholl was convinced it was a minor setback. He'd been out of the game for a few years so all it was going to take was another opportunity. Atholl was sure these trips abroad were the best way of ensuring he accomplished his task. If what he had seen in Vienna was anything to go by, the chaos of these football matches allowed a person to get away with anything, including murder. And yet. Atholl put from his mind any doubts over his actions. He had been brought up with a clear sense of duty throughout his life. His duty to the army had been exemplary, after a fashion, and he wished the same to be said with regard to his attitude to his family name and the McClackit heritage.

The next morning he asked his secretary to get a full list of fixtures from the football association of Scotland. As he looked at the next couple of games he saw they were back to back away games in Latvia and Estonia. He sat up at this as he had recently been discussing with the MD the possibility of moving into the Baltics with their security service operations. Various tales of Russian mafia kidnapping and robberies had gripped the imagination of the British press and he thought there might be some business opportunities available.

He asked his secretary to get Bryce, his managing director, on the phone.

"Bryce, it's Atholl. How's things? Get down to Quinns at the weekend?"

"Hi Atholl, yes I did get down but it was grim. Bloody Bath, will those west country bumpkins ever get any worse. It's just not on. What can I do you for?"

"I've just been reviewing the conversation we had about the Baltics last month and was looking to take a trip out in October, have a scout around a couple of places, Riga, Tallinn. I was thinking of posing as a UK businessman looking to invest but worried about protection. I can get a few quotes on the competition and see how they match up with the services we offer. Really dipping a toe in the water sort of thing."

"Sounds good. Draw up an itinerary with a couple of objectives, just to make it look official, and I'll sign it off. Any other ideas, just let me know as we're looking to get out of Africa as much as possible. These places are virtually round the corner compared to the likes of Angola and Nigeria. You up for a game of squash Thursday lunchtime?"

"Sounds good."

"Excellent. See you at 12.30"

At the sound of the tone, Atholl realised why Bryce had been so good in the SAS. He was prepared to think differently and was always looking for a new way of doing things. Riga here I come he thought.

Chapter 7

Latvia Loca

DOMINIC FRASER APPEARED in Paddy Whelans, Riga's finest Irish bar, a bulky carrier bag under his right arm. The bar was full of Scotland fans taking advantage of the cheap Latvian prices. There was a wee bit of a bottleneck at the front but when you pressed on into the bar it opened out. The pub had clearly been bought in a pub supermarket, definitely in the Irish shop/bar section. He saw Kenny Bradley and Gus McSween in a booth and wandered over. Dominic was the editor of the Scotland fanzine, Sporran Legion, and a long time acquaintance of Kenny and Gus's. The Spice Girls "Wannabe" was blaring out of the pub sound system but still couldn't totally drown the hubbub of noise coming from the fans.

"Alright lads?" said Dominic.

"No, no really" said Kenny "Just had a wee bit of aggro wi' some locals"

"What? That's no like you"

"All, ah'll say is we didnae start it. Just had to calm Rambo down a bit before he started World War III." said Gus who was clearly enjoying taking the moral high ground for once.

"They burnt ma hat, they fucking set fire to my hat and burnt it," said Kenny, an anguished tone creeping into his voice. His attempt to get taken seriously wasn't helped by the fact that he was wearing a tartan baseball cap which had a piece of plastic stuck on its front, the bit of plastic having "Think Scottish" printed on it.

"Who did this? They honestly set fire to his hat?" Dominic asked Gus.

"Aye, unfortunately he wisnae wearin it at the time, like. It was the hat he bought in Red Square last year. This old boy from Stonehaven came over and told us a couple o locals were upset at Kenny wearing a Russian hat. He suggested Kenny take his baseball cap and he'd look after the cossack bunnet. We went to see Frances Fairweather at her hotel to say hello and came back 30 minutes later to find out these two Latvian boys had started usin the hat as an ashtray, then taken it outside and gone the whole fuckin' hog, like, makin' a wee bonfire out of numbnuts' hat. He's no a happy camper by the way, so go easy on the poor wee soul."

"Ach, shut it you. If this isn't bad enough on its own, I've to listen to you getting on your high horse and telling me I was in the wrong. I accept that and all I will say in my defence is after I called him a fucking Latvian homosexual bastard, I did offer to buy him a drink. Once I had cooled down." Kenny felt he had gone a bit over the top towards the end especially when he realised the size of the locals involved.

"Sure it wasne once your hat had cooled down," said Gus, an evil grin on his face. "Ah've always had you down as a bit of a hothead, like".

"So did they have a drink wi you?" asked Dominic who was bemused by the whole story but had to admit, he'd never seen Kenny so worked up.

"Well one did but his mate was less than chuffed over the homosexual remark. I think he still wants to kill me judging by the stares he's given me." At this last remark, Kenny nodded towards a large blond youth sitting at the bar who was giving him the evil eye.

"Christ, Kenny, you know how to pick them. He looks like Dolph Lundgren's big brother."

"Aye well Dominic, if bigmouth strikes again, he knows he can always count on us for back up. We'll no leave you stranded Kenny whatever the cost to our personal well bein, like" said Gus.

"Magic, that's me well protected then"

"You could always call Harold for a bit of back up if things get really nasty" suggested Dominic in a less than convincing tone of voice.

"Christ, this just gets better and better. First, my hat gets burnt then you two come up with ideas like calling up Harold and the boys. Get fuckin' real. Anyway, forget about man mountain over there and concentrate on the night. How's sales Dominic?"

"No bad, bordering on complete shite."

You still floggin that comic?" asked Gus.

"No, essentially I am just carrying around seventy five copies around Riga and allowing Scotland fans to tell me to fuck off when I ask them if they want to buy a copy".

"That good?" asked Kenny.

"Aye, that fucken good. You'd think I was askin' them to cut off their right arm as opposed to coughin up a pound."

"Just as well we're subscribers, like" said Gus

"You? A fucking subscriber? Don't make me laugh. Kenny subscribes and you read his copy, you tight wee cunt. That barmaid in Amsterdam couldnae have been as tight as you."

"Hey! Where you'd hear about her?"

"Hey! Never reveal your sources" said Dominic "but from what I heard you got more than you bargained for"

"What the fuck do you mean by that?" exploded Gus worried his secret was out.

"Does the word "ladyboy" mean anything do you?"

"Get tae fuck man, no way, no fucking way Jose"

"Aye well, don't let the truth get in the way o' a good story," replied Dominic. "What you's up to tonight?"

"Well I believe there's a gallery opening tonight in the old town so we may well take that in before going to admire some outdooor sculptures in a forest whilst the sun sets to the sounds of a live classical string quartet." said Kenny.

"Just getting gassed then?" replied Dominic.

"Too fucken right" said Gus. "Ah've heard enough pish about art the day to do me a lifetime."

"What the fuck are you on about? You're about as artistic as my last fart" said Dominic.

"Funny you should say that as it reminds me of a conversation earlier today regarding art and wind," said Kenny. "Gus here is the man for the beauty and pain of classical art, aren't you my fat little friend."

"Hey, ah wisnae tae know ah was sittin next to the world's most intelligent burd."

"This sounds good" says Dominic.

"Good, this is better than good. Our friend here, as is his wont, decided to impress the female passenger next to him on the plane over. Give's it the usual chat, "you travelling on business or on holiday?", "where you from? thought I recognised the accent,", "how long you staying?" and then the best bit comes right at the end when he asks her what she does. "Actually I'm a curator for the Guggenheim museum in Venice and I'm on my way to pick up piece of art by the Latvian artist Laartu" she replies.

To which fannybaws here goes, "Oh really, I'm a bit of art fan myself but mainly the classical stuff, I don't know a lot but I know what I like."

"No way" said Dominic. "I don't know a lot but ah know what ah like. Classic."

"To this she goes "Fantastic, who is your favourite artist?" So here it comes, the piece de fucking resistance "My favourite artist is Mistral, though mainly the early period." comes the reply. "Mistral?" she goes, "isn't that the wind?"

So Gus goes, "No, no, ah know where you're coming from but this guy was a real classical painter, like. They did a TV programme about him when ah was younger, it was a dramaticisation of his life, and he was played by that American boy that did the time for a wee bit of Charlie, as they say. What the fu… what was his name again? Peach, no Keach, Stacey Keach. He was such a good actor cos he always got his lines straight"

"So I'm sitting there thinking he's got this wrong," says Kenny. "I couldn't fucking place it but then it clicked. He's thinking of "Mistrals Daughter", a mini series from the 80's based on somebody like Matisse or some other French painter. I try to point this out but he's not having it, talk about when you're in a hole stop digging, so he goes on trying to tell this American bird he's always admired Mistral and his fucking early period but can never seem to find any of his works in the museums he's visited."

"When the fuck were you last in a museum?" said Dominic

"Last year in Moscow for the Russia game, you cheeky bastard"

"What? To use the gents for free?"

"And what if ah was? 30p for a shite in one o they tardis things in the street. Get that tae fuck man."

"A point well put, young Gus." Kenny looked down the bar just in time to see Andy Muir's had bobbing up and down around the bar. "Aye, aye, here's our journo pal from Vienna. Must still be doing research on the wonders of the Tartan Army. You should have a word with him Dominic, he might be able to plug the comic."

"Not a bad idea Kenny. Who does he write for?"

"He's freelance. Says he's going to try and get a piece in the New Yorker or Harpers and Queen, an upmarket look at down market guys."

"Hey, there's nothing downmarket about me ya tube. It's only top quality burds that are after me, like." said Gus

"Just like the one on the plane I suppose" said Kenny.

At this Andy Muir approached, shaking himself free from the scrum at the bar. "All right chaps, who wants a drink? Expenses are still looking good, so the milky bars are on me."

"No problem Andy," said Gus "good to see you again, especially when you're buyin. Come on I'll gie you a hand at the bar, my good man. Lagers all round or whatever the local pish is?". Getting a quick nod from the remaining two Andy and Gus headed off to the bar of Paddy Whelan's.

"That bloke's a journo?" asked Dominic.

"Says he is," said Kenny "Why do you ask?".

"It's just that all the ones I've met have been tighter than a duck's arse. The idea of them spending any more of their expenses than they have to is fucking odd. If he's spending it on fans that's even more incredible".

"It's funny you should say that as a couple of things don't quite add up about the cunt. He hasn't got a card with his contact details and has always stayed clear of the tartan hack pack despite me offering to introduce him to the ones I know. Still, he's no doing anyone any harm but something's no quite right, maybe its just because he's a posh Scot"

"A posh Scot!" Dominic exploded. "Those wanks get right on my nerves. Ok, I'll catch you later, I'm going to see if anybody else in this bar doesn't want a fanzine". Dominic walked off to the far end of the bar to another table of fans just as Gus and Andy came back with the drinks.

"What happened to him?" said Gus. "John Menzies gie him a call for another ten copies?"

"He's just away to try and punt some more copies. He'll be back in a minute," Kenny replied. The sound system was now pumping out "Firestarter" by the Prodigy and the place was definitely warming up.

Gus had a big smile on his face. "Hear that Kenny, special request from yours truly."

"Very fucking funny," said Kenny who proceeded to explain to Andy what had happened earlier on.

"Ok chaps, now we've broken the ice with the locals, what's the plan for tonight?" asked Andy.

"A bit quieter than the last time Andy, got the father in law with me," said Kenny.

"Where is he now?" said Andy

"He's, eh, looking into a possible business opportunity." came an unconvincing answer from Kenny, who had managed to forget all about Harold and his Baltic enterprises.

"Your father in law a big Scotland fan?" asked Andy.

"No, he hates football. More of a golfer actually. It's the usual Scottish story in that you could be a bit of a nutter, play off scratch and everybody would think you were slightly misunderstood. As it happens, my father-in-law is a crazed lunatic and does play off scratch but I wouldn't advise you to call him misunderstood, should you be unfortunate enough to meet him"

"Calm down Kenny," said Gus, "Walls have ears." The alcohol was having more of an effect on Kenny than Gus, who knew it wasn't wise to mouth off about Harold on an away trip.

"Fair point," said Kenny.

Kenny looked around Paddy Whelans trying to put any thoughts of Harold MacMillan out of his head. Harold had spoken to him briefly at the airport when they arrived in Riga. He'd told Kenny he'd speak to him at more length in Tallinn. After that he had disappeared into a long black Mercedes which was waiting for him outside the terminal building and sped off into the night. Kenny had not heard from him since and presumed he would be making his own way to Estonia.

Turning his mind back to the present, he looked around him. The bar was pretty mobbed with Scots and he could see a couple of guys already making inroads with the local females.

"Anything caught your eye?" he asked Andy.

"Well, I was at the Independence Monument earlier on

today watching the changing of the guard and did you know those two large buildings further along the river were actually Zeppelin hangars but are now cheese and meat markets" said Andy.

Gus snorted, "Funnily enough ah don't really make much of an effort to get to cheese markets when ah'm on tour," he said.

"Aye but you've been to enough meat markets" said Kenny, a grin on his face.

"Shut it you!"

"That kind of sight wasn't exactly what I was talking about Andy" said Kenny.

"No?"

"Fucks sake Andy man, get a grip," Gus went on "he's talkin about Hugh McIlvanney, talent, burds. And as it happens in this place ahm right in ma element, like, and ah can see a vision of loveliness even as ah speak."

"Tell me it's not that big dark headed thing sitting at the bar. Talk about quantity not quality." said Kenny.

"Hey, she's a love machine pal" replied Gus in a gleeful tone.

"Love machine? It looks like she's just come out of one of those zeppelin hangars Andy was talking about"

"Leave it to me, my man," said Gus getting up from the table and running his hands through his hair transplant, trying to get it under control. The music now playing was Fast Love by George Michael. "You'd better get a move on wee man, now they're playing your tune," said Kenny.

"What if she doesn't speak English?" asked Andy astonished at what he was seeing.

"It doesn't matter, I'm fluent in the language of love, and romance is my middle name. Angus Romance McSween. Don't wait up."

Andy watched amazed as Gus casually strolled up to a woman who was a foot taller than him and at least twice his weight. He had listened intently to Kenny's tale of the hat burning. He was slightly concerned about the local youth's attitude and considered what he might have to do if it turned nasty. Was he going to have to protect someone he was trying to kill?

"How does he do it?" he asked Kenny.

"It's a percentage game, ask enough Robbie Fowlers and one of them is bound to say yes. You should get all the gory details off him tomorrow. You might get an article for Penthouse out of it, "My Night of Passion with Liga from Riga" or "My Latvian Lover Loved Me and Left". Maybe that's got too many L's. Anyway, you're the journalist, I am sure you can come up with something a bit snappier".

"Yes, if you say so. Where are you staying in Riga?" asked Andy, trying to get the conversation back on semi normal lines.

"We're staying at a half renovated hotel called the Victoria or Victorija. The renovated half is very nice but unfortunately they have still to work their way down to ours on the first floor. The plumbing is bad as we don't have an en suite so you've got to walk down the corridor for a pee and as for the electrics, don't get me started."

At this Andy's ears pricked up. "Is it the same the UK where if you're on the first floor your room number begins with a one. I had heard say there was going to be some old baboushka type on each floor who would only present you with your room key after you had shown your passport."

"No, it's no that bad. There's a reception but when I've asked for the key they've just ended up giving it to you without asking for ID. Where are you staying, by the way?" replied Kenny.

"Eh, the SAS Radisson across the river." said Atholl

"Nice one. Those expenses must just be rolling in to cover you for that. Is that not where the squad is staying?"

"Yes, I believe so" confirmed Andy. That explained why those small thin chaps with Scotland tracksuits in the Radisson coffee shop had taken exception to him asking them if they supported the team at every match. They were the team.

He had to think quickly to try and get Kenny's room number. "Funnily enough I asked for a room on the first floor at my hotel, 18 is my lucky number you see so I was hoping that they could see their way to giving me it but everything goes from 100 up. What number have you got in the Victorija?"

"Close but no cigar, we're in room 11."

"Excellent" thought Andy. Just as he'd worked out where this left him, a large presence loomed over the table. The hat burning youth from earlier on had finally drunk enough to tip him over the edge and into confrontational mood.

"You" he said pointing an unsteady finger at Kenny. "You Scottish fucking Scottish homo". At this he took a step forward and Andy managed to stick his leg out in time to trip up the guy. The Latvian put his arms out to stop his fall but Andy managed to grab one arm and pull him down whilst trying to make it look like he was helping him. Blood spurted across the table as the youth's nose hit the edge.

"Oops, somebody had one beer too many" said Andy as the bar staff came over to sort out the mess. The Latvian was dragged to his feet whilst a barman clutched a towel across his face to try and stem the blood flow. The manager asked if everyone was ok and cleaned up the table.

"Shall we move?" suggested Andy.

"Anything you say" said Kenny who was a bit stunned by what he had just witnessed.

"Actually, I'm sorry but maybe I had better leave. I am going to cruise a few more bars and try and get some more background stuff for the comics, will probably see you at the game tomorrow." said Andy who didn't really want to draw anymore attention to himself.

"Aye, no problem, Andy. We'll be in this bar or around here somewhere. The stadium's no that far out so we'll probably just jump in a taxi. Catch you later".

Kenny was relieved he'd gone. There was something not right about Andy Muir but he just couldn't put his finger on it. That last incident had left a bad taste. He knew he had it coming as he'd gone over the top in insulting the guy but he certainly seemed to give his head a fair old crack on that table.

Atholl left Paddy Whelans and turned right down Grecinieku Street. He had seen a taxi rank at the bottom of the street and wanted to move quickly to get the job done. He felt on a bit of a high after the scene in the bar, the old skills not completely forgotten. Atholl walked on down the street which was extremely dark. It appeared only twenty five percent of the streetlights were actually functioning. He walked into a couple of elderly guys in kilts who were deep in negotiation with a couple of hookers, it was so dark. He apologised but as he was walking on heard one of the men remark, "Come on doll, why don't Jock and I take you and your pal for a wee drink and get to know each other better." Life in the old dog yet thought

Atholl. He could see the cab rank at the end of the street so picked up his pace. The door of the first cab in the rank was slightly ajar and he pulled it open and jumped in saying "Hotel Victorija, please".

* * * * *

Kenny had had enough. It had been half an hour since Andy left and there was only so much shite you could talk about the Scotland team. The earlier incident was preying on his mind as well. The team was picking itself these days and they were hoping to build on the result in Vienna, even with Darren Jackson in the squad. A couple of guys suggested a brothel which featured in the alternative Riga guidebook but having seen a guy's arse smoking a cigar earlier on Kenny knew he had seen it all. The incident with the cigar was very amusing. Some wee squat barrel of a guy had passed out in what could loosely be termed Paddy Whelans beer garden. After the Tadger Currie incident Kenny had made sure the guy was alive but he just wanted a kip by the sound of his mutterings so Kenny left him face down on a picnic table contraption. It was then that some comedian had lifted his kilt and put a Castella sized cigar between the cheeks of his arse. He had lit the cigar and then used the guys bum cheeks like a bellows to get a light going. It was all going really well and a crowd had developed to see the arse smoke a cigar. Sadly, all had not ended well when the cigar fell out of his crack and set light to his anal hair. A kindly volunteer had thrown the remnants of his pint over the inferno before it got out of hand and set fire to his kilt but sleeping beauty was less than impressed when he pointedly remarked, "Just trying to get a wee kip and some cunt sets fire tae ma pubes. Its not on, its just not on."

98

"Aw right, am for the off," said Kenny.

"Ye taking Casanova wi ye?" asked Dominic who had returned on Andy's departure.

Kenny turned and looked up the bar to see Gus and his new girlfriend snogging the face off each other whilst sitting at the bar.

"Good God, is he still at it? I spoke to him in the gents and he said he's going back to her place. The worrying thing is she has said she's up for anything and if any of you boys want a shot, please feel free."

"You're kidding. You'd need to roll her in flour to find the wet spot" said Dominic.

"Sadly, I am not joking. I think he's spread the word around and they've found another couple of desperadoes for their posse. I'm off to my kip and to prepare myself for tomorrow."

"What you've got a big day ahead?" asked Dominic.

"No to prepare myself for his tales of sexual depravity. I'm away to see if he can take his tongue out of her mouth for long enough to say cheerio."

After he left Paddy Whelan's, Kenny wandered down Avenue Kaka towards the Victorija. He'd thought about getting a taxi but was desparate for a slash once the cold night air hit him so he'd gone up a close to relieve himself. On coming out of the alley he'd nearly bumped into a group of Shetlanders he knew and considered it a close escape. Those guys were truly mental once they got on the bevvy. He remembered the story of one of them who'd shagged his hotel cleaner for 40 dollars the year before in Moscow. Unreal. Riga had to be one of the most poorly lit cities he'd ever been to. The smell of cheap diesel filled his nostrils as he kept walking at a steady pace. He tripped a couple of times on broken paving slabs. Anyone watching this must think I'm totally blootered he thought. He wondered if a taxi would have been a better option but the streets were as quiet as they were dark. Bizarrely, as he walked past a taxi, which had stopped at the traffic lights, he thought he saw Andy Muir sitting in the back. It had taken him a few seconds to accustom his eyes to the gloom but by that time the lights had changed and the taxi was gone. Funny thing was, it was heading back into town. Andy said he was going to cruise a few more bars but didn't say anything about going out of the city centre. Maybe he'd been tipped off about somewhere out of town and it was closed.

Kenny was just walking up to the hotel when a taxi pulled up outside. The passengers were two elderly gentlemen in kilts plus two twenty something bottle blondes with tight red tops, black mini skirts and those spangly tights favoured by Eastern European hookers. As one of the men turned round he saw Kenny and shouted out "Kenny bloody Bradley! How you doin?"

"Not nearly as well as you Jock Paisley, you ugly old git." Jock Paisley was another old time pal of Kenny's. Jock went way back to the nightmare trip that was Brussels in 1962 when the greatest Scotland team never to play in a World Cup had blown a play off with Czechoslovakia. He'd been a regular through the good times and the bad times, including Argentina. Kenny never knew where he got the stamina from and sometimes wondered if this would be him in 30 years.

"Hey son, come on. They're practically givin it away and at these prices it would be rude not to. I need a word actually, well more than a word. Harry here has got first rights on our room.

Is there any chance you could give me your room for an hour. Go to the bar, have a nightcap and put it on our tab. I'll come and have a drink with you when I'm done. What do you say?"

"Jock, come on. I just want my kip but...well as it's you. It's room 11. I'll go and get the key. It's a twin room so take the bed closest to the window as that's Gus's. He won't be using it tonight, that's for certain. Come on, I'll get the key."

The receptionist gave Kenny a funny look when he asked for the key but handed it over. Kenny passed it to Jock saying "Ok, one hour, the meter's running and I'll see you in the bar."

Kenny went up to the hotel bar on the first floor. Whoever took the photos of these places for hotel brochures must be a genius with a camera, he thought. What had appeared in the promotional pamphlet as a wide homely bar, with a large selection of drinks now looked like something you would see in the bar of a Highland caravan park. The furnishings looked like they'd been liberated from a Victorian sauna. The solitary poster of Riga featured the zeppelin hangars reminding Kenny of Gus and his night of passion ahead. I knew he liked team sports, thought Kenny, but that was going too far.

Continuing to scan round the bar, he saw one lager pump, three bottles of vodka and one dodgy Latvian whisky. The night porter looked extremely hacked off at having to serve Kenny a beer so Kenny consoled himself with the thought that this boy had seen nothing yet. It was two am but the night was young for most of the Tartan Army. He would he would be getting more, not less, custom as the night wore on and the troops drifted back.

Kenny had taken a couple of sips of the lager he'd ordered and was thinking more about Jock Paisley and the remarkable stamina of the guy. All of a sudden there was a flickering of the lights in the bar followed by a loud scream. The night porter stuck his head round the door of his restroom. He looked enquiringly at Kenny, clearly waiting for a response that would mean he could go back to sleep and pretend nothing was wrong.

"Sorry pal, but I think I just heard someone scream," said Kenny in apologetic tone. Suddenly footsteps came crashing down the staircase and Kenny saw a blur of gold, black and red flash past the door to the bar. He thought it might be one of the girls who had been with Jock and his mate but which one. His room was closer to reception than Jock's which was on the fourth floor so it must be Jock's girl who was doing a runner. But why?

Kenny ran up the stairs to the first floor and looked down the corridor to his room. The prone figure of Jock Paisley lay half in and half out of the room. There was a smell of burnt flesh, which grew stronger the closer he got to Jock. He reached down but he could see it was too late.

The night porter had finally appeared and looked down at Jock then up at Kenny. "Ambulance?" he asked.

"Nope, I don't know what Latvian is for undertaker but that's what you're going to need. So no, no ambulance"

* * * * *

Atholl sat in the bar of the SAS Radisson Riga drinking a brandy. It had turned a bit nippy out so he felt in need of warmth and comfort. Might even run an eye over the hookers later, he thought. After all, he was on expenses. He laughed at his own joke. Those guys were two of thickest individuals he had ever met. All you had to do was tell them you were from a paper or a mag and they would just roll over for you. He'd tried it on another couple of fans with exactly the same results. Outstanding. He'd had no difficulty getting the key to room 11 from the receptionist who had hardly taken her eyes from a Latvian soap on her TV whilst she had given him the key. He had known what he wanted to do as soon as Kenny Bradley mentioned poor electrics in the hotel. He'd unscrewed the main light switch in room 11. To make matters better it was a double switch, one switch for the bathroom and one switch for the bedroom. He then connected the live wires to the switch itself. He'd held the wire in place with a small piece of matchstick. Once the light was switched on, the switch itself would become live but the wire would come free after the small bit of wood had been burnt off and it would look like genuinely loose faulty wiring. A small bit of accelerant on the switch added to the overall effect.

It had worked once before in Northern Ireland when an informant had been getting a bit mouthy and asking for more money than he was worth. No prizes for originality, but never mind. He hadn't wanted to stay on in Latvia but thought it might look a bit odd if he disappeared. The thought of another night in Riga did little for him but there were certain comforts available to make life a little more bearable. Hell, he might even go to the game. He was Scottish after all. Ha ha, Christ two jokes in one night. He was on fire and speaking of hot, who was this vision approaching. "Is there anything I can get for you, sir?" she asked in heavily accented English.

"Yes, I dare say there is," replied Atholl reaching for his room key

* * * * *

Atholl had felt he was losing control for the first time in his life. The following morning he had gone for walk round Riga. It was matchday and he was planning to stay away from the main drag, especially Paddy Whelans pub where he expected most of the fans to be gathering. He couldn't go back to the Victorija hotel in case he was recognised but he needed to get verification on whether or not his job was done.

He was walking across the main bridge over the Daugava into the old town when he recognised a Scotland fan coming towards him. He couldn't be sure but he thought it was someone he might have seen the previous night with Kenny and Gus. The guy seemed to be doing his best to ignore him but he had to get confirmation he had been successful in removing Kenny Bradley.

"Hello" he said cheerily as the chap approached. "It's Dominic isn't it?"

"Aye, hello, how ye doin?" came an unenthusiastic reply.

"Out getting some air before the game, trying to blow the cobwebs away. You?" replied Atholl.

"I'm just going to see Frances Fairweather at the team hotel," said Dominic

"Oh yes. Who's he?"

"It's not a he, she's a she." said Dominic in an exasperated tone. "She runs the supporters club, I've got a bit of bad news for her about a fan."

Atholl thought at last, he's gone. "Nothing serious I trust" said Atholl.

"No, its serious all right, fucken terminal to be honest. One of the fans was killed last night in an accident in the hotel. Bit of faulty wiring on a light switch and he was electrocuted. No that big a shock but given his age it was enough to prove fatal. Or so they think, I'm no expert," came the reply from Dominic.

"What do you mean given his age?" demanded Atholl, this didn't sound like what he was expecting to hear.

"It was an old guy called Jock Paisley. He was in his 60's, was a heavy smoker, had a wee heart attack last year so was susceptible to something pushing him over the edge. Worst thing was, it wasnae even his room. He'd borrowed the room key off Kenny as he had a hooker wi' him. Kenny and Gus are pretty shook up."

"You are telling me Kenny Bradley is still alive?" said Atholl in a quiet voice.

"Aye and it's thanks to amazing Grace" replied Dominic.

"What are you talking about?" said Atholl, the sudden understanding of another failed mission coming down hard.

"Well, that was the name of the hooker Jock had met, Grace. If it hadn't been for her it would have been Kenny that walked in and turned the light on. I've got to crack on as we tried to phone Frances but I think she's in a security meeting so she needs to be told in person. She might be able to get in touch with his family back home. Catch you later if you're still around."

The bridge was broad and open to the elements. As a chill wind blew down the Daugava river Atholl realised he had to get a grip. Losing control at this stage would not help him or the McClackit clan. He had to identify where he had gone wrong and clarify his new objective. He started walking towards the old town. As he crossed the road at the end of the bridge he saw a coffee house, He went in and ordered a brandy and an espresso. Sitting at the window gazing out at the river he began to put together his earlier strategies and see where they had failed him. One of his strengths in Northern Ireland was that he had never become overly confident. That was helped to a large extent by the fact the amount of time he spent in the Six Counties was minimal. He often wondered if the IRA and UDA would have been amused to find he spent most of his time in the Republic posing as a gay antique dealer, only nipping across the border as required. He reviewed what he had attempted to do in Vienna and Riga, realising the flaw in both cases, lack of control at the point of completion. The deed had not been done by his own hands but if that was what it took then so be it. It had been a few years since he'd got his hands dirty at the sharp end of the business but needs must.

* * * * *

The train had been moving for about four hours after leaving Riga station. Atholl sat back on the carriage seat and looked out at the bleak Latvian countryside. After the brandy and coffee earlier on, he'd returned to his hotel managing to avoid any more Scotland fans. He'd checked out and made enquiries as to how one might get to Tallinn. The air prices were prohibitive, even on company expenses, but the train sounded a more reasonable method of travel despite it taking seven hours. He'd thought a quick escape from Riga might be in his best interests in case the hotel receptionist at the Victorija gave a description of him to the police. He'd managed to get a seat on the lunchtime train and was surprised how quiet it was, even though it was a Saturday.

The view from the windows was unchanging, a low flat plain interspersed with forests dominated the landscape as far as the eye could see. There was no livestock in the fields, the whole vista denuded of life. He'd dozed off it was so boring only to be shaken awake by a border guard demanding to see his passport. He was obviously back on good form as he'd bent the guard's wrist backwards before he realised he wasn't being attacked. The guard was a spotty teenager whose shock at such treatment left him too scared to go and complain to a senior officer.

Once his passport was stamped, the guard using his other hand to complete the job, Atholl tried to calm down with some breathing exercises his ex wife had taught him. They were going well until he remembered they were part of her warm up exercises for tantric sex. As he was faced with another three hours on the train Atholl stopped the breathing exercises. He didn't think it was pragmatic to spend a railway journey in a foreign country with an erection that might last the best part of ninety minutes.

To take his mind off all matters of a sexual nature he thought about the Scotland fans he had met so far on his travels. He was part of them but they appeared to come from another Scotland to the one he knew but then again, how well did he know Scotland? His view of the country was dominated by family and clan gatherings, summer balls on the big estates, loch side barbecues with freshly caught fish and regimental dances. All this, plus the odd shooting weekend in autumn, hardly exposed him to the country and its people as a whole. To most of the fans he met, the idea of barbecued meat revolved around a well done kebab once the pubs had closed.

His thoughts moved on to his father and Castle McClackit. He had no real attachment to the place but found it hard to think of actually letting it go. No doubt the few remaining McClackits would emerge from under their stones in Virginia and Tasmania to protest against anything he did. Distant cousin Lionel in Richmond, Virginia would be the biggest problem given his complete devotion to the clan and all things McClackit. Atholl realised how far from grace the clan had fallen when its biggest supporter was a southern bigot chiropodist who believed George Washington, Henry Ford, Marilyn Monroe and Elvis Presley were all clan McClackit descendants.

Thinking about it in these terms, Atholl had no desire to live in Scotland and be hounded by these distant clan members. The quicker he got rid of the castle once his father pegged it, the better. This thought reminded him to contact an Aberdeen estate agent with regards to getting it valued. He would make sure Potter and the other estate workers were looked after but that would be it. Protecting the family name by killing Bradley would be one thing, living in Scotland would be another.

The train pulled into Tallinn station at 7pm. Atholl walked out of the station and jumped in a cab. He suddenly realised he didn't have a clue where he wanted to go. So much for planning ahead he thought. Clearly he'd got too confident, believing he would complete the job in Riga.

"Hotel?" asked the taxi driver.

"You know hotel?" asked Atholl

"Hotel Viru, good hotel" came the reply.

"Hotel Viru it is then" said Atholl and the taxi drove off in the gathering gloom.

Chapter 8

Magical Mystery Tour

"FUCK'S SAKE MAN, more fuckin trees. This journey is never endin and the scenery is complete shite, like. The brochure never said it would be like this. Pass me another lager Dominic, it's only bevvy that's goin to get me through this. Hey, did ye see the match programme the other night? The printing was rotten man, it was semi fuckin legible like."

"Should be all right for you Gus" said Dominic

"How's that then?"

"You're semi fuckin literate," said Dominic passing a can of lager to the seat in front of him.

"Well done smart arse! You been sittin there thinkin these side splitters all the way up from Riga?" came a less than impressed reply.

Gus McSween was sitting at the window on a 52 seater coach travelling up to Tallinn from the Estonian-Latvian border. They had been on the bus for six hours but that included a three hour stop at the border where a supposed computer malfunction had halted their journey.

"Ah told ye that guy Brian should have offered the border guard bastard a bribe" said Gus after he'd opened the can of lager and taken a slug.

"I think it was the offer of a bribe that caused the problem" replied Kenny.

"Naw, it wisnae, it was the size of the bribe. Ye've got to think like these Baltic cunts think. If you bale up in a 52 seater and only offer a bribe, suitable for a four door saloon, Tatu the border guard is goin to think we're taking the piss. And he'd be right. If ah was runnin this bus we'd be sittin in the Hell Hunt having a pint of Guinness and a shepherd's pie"

"If you'd been running this bus we'd still be in Riga," said Dominic. "Given the fact you had to be physically carried onto the bus you were so out of it, what the fuck could you have organised?"

"Alright, smart bastard, ah take yer point" said Gus. "Ah was drinkin to Jock Paisley, like. That Jagermeister's fuckin rocket fuel by the way. And to think ah only had the three."

"Aye, three pints" was the reply from Dominic. "You've got a point about this scenery though man. What a dull country this is. Flat bit of barren land then trees, another flat bit of land then more fucking trees, god knows what its like in the depths of winter. Mind you if it looks dull outside, the view of the inside of this bus is positively frightening. Maybe they were calling for reinforcements at the border and that's what the hold up was."

They were on the bus courtesy of a conversation in the Hotel Victorija Kenny had held with another Scotland fan called Brian who came from a mining village just outside Nottingham. The guy had told him there was a group of sixteen from his village who had booked up. They were all miners from Fife who had moved down after the last pits closed in Scotland. The bus that picked them up at the airport in Riga was a fifty two seater when they had been expecting a mini bus. He had asked the driver if it was the same bus that would take them to Tallinn and he had said yes. Brian told Kenny he didn't see any problem in them hopping on board as the trip was paid for and all they would have to do is give the driver a few bob to keep him happy. As they were all staying in the same hotel this had been the dream ticket, until Gus, on the back of his Jagermeister frenzy, had invited every Scotland fan in the hotel on the bus trip north to Tallinn.

Their party of sixteen plus Kenny, Gus and Dominic had now swelled to approximately 46. Brian the bus organiser had taken it remarkably well and commented, "The more the merrier, plus it will be less for you boys to chip in to keep the driver sweet"

A carry out big enough to sink a battleship had been loaded on board and they were off. When he finally awoke, Gus had perked up considerably when he discovered there were women on board. The fact there were only three and they were all with boyfriends hardly registered.

"Had many a good time with burds on busses down to Blackpool and back on the September weekend. Oh yes, ahm a maestro at the mobile shaggin like. Ah was always one to enjoy a good bus ride if you get my drift. Even better on the trains mind, well, it used to be. Since they've introduced those airplane type carriages its no sae good. When you're on a train its no got quite the same cachet to ask a burd if she'd like to join the five feet high club."

"Did you just use the word cachet" asked an incredulous Dominic Fraser.

"Aye ah did fannybaws. Think you're the only Guardian reading twat with an education on this bus? Get tae fuck. As ah was saying those six seater carriages with the sliding doors were the best, like. Let the train take the strain indeed. Ah remember that time we got the overnight train to Cardiff in 1979, eh Kenny? Ah met this runaway from an orphanage in Northern Ireland. Ah wis only 17 at the time, she must have been 16 going on 46. She was up for anythin, like. After half an hour o' my silver tongue, she had her silver tongue wrapped round a certain part o' my anatomy and ahm no talking about ma big toe. Those older guys we were wi were spewin as they thought they should have had first go like, age giving them seniority, but she wasnae interested in them. She wanted the youth squad, no the coaching staff wi old heads on old shoulders."

"So you're telling me that within half an hour of meeting this girl, she'd blown you?" said an astonished Dominic.

"Aye, as God or Kenny Bradley is my witness."

"Talk about sad but true!" Kenny said "What made it worse was just before she got off in Birmingham she told me she'd really fancied me but as I hadn't made a move, she'd taken second best. I thought the day couldn't get any worse then we got gubbed 3-0 by a fuckin John Toshack hat trick. Got back to Dumfries at 5 am on the Sunday morning. A complete nightmare. No sleep for two nights and young Lochinvar here telling everybody he met he was in love with a runaway who had runaway with his heart. She'd given him her phone number you see and he tried it when he got back. You know who answered it?

"No, go on?"

"The office receptionist at Belfast Dogs Home."

"Ha fucking ha. You two are well suited, like. Losers in love the pair of you. The last time either of you cunts had a ride there was a Labour government in power and Abba were number 1. Where the fuck are we now? Is he stoppin? Wait a minute, is that the sea?" said Gus in an excited tone.

The driver had pulled over for what was described by Brian as a quick piss stop. The bus emptied quickly but not nearly as quickly as the bladders that had been storing cheap Latvian lager for the past hour. Above the smell of piss, Kenny could smell the sea and decided to have a look. After walking through a small wooded area found himself on a long, desolate beach. A biting wind blew sand in his face and he was about to turn back when he saw Gus sitting on the sand, taking off his socks and shoes.

"Are you about to do what I think you are?"

"Too right man. Cannae come to the beach and no have a paddle, like." replied Gus.

He's off his fucking head thought Kenny as its baltic by the Baltic. He'd heard somewhere about the Baltic Riviera and presumed it was a wind up but this was a beautiful stretch of coast. He was thinking of joining Gus for a laugh but then Brian shouted at them from the edge of the trees.

"Come on, we've wasted enough time at that fucking border if we're to get there before the pubs shut. For fucks sake don't go for a paddle Gus, we're out o here."

"Logic like that ye cannae argue wi" Gus replied. "Pubs closing versus freezin my nuts off in the Baltic is a no brainer. Come on you, get back on the bus pronto."

Kenny spent the rest of the journey trying to sleep. It had

been a nightmare bus journey and he couldn't wait to get to his bed. He'd been in Tallinn once before in 1994. He'd missed the Scotland game there in 1993 to go to Portugal instead. Talk about making a wrong choice. They'd been totally gubbed 5-0 in Lisbon, the game had been referred to by some as the night a team died. Then, Scotland had played in Tallinn in May and apparently it had been the trip of a lifetime. A town totally unused to westerners, cheap bevvy, loads of gorgeous women, a truly magical place with a Disneyesque old town. He'd even heard they didn't have sellotape, shopgirls wrapped all the purchases in brown paper and tied them up with string. The only plus was that Gus had missed it as well. They had,however made a trip in 1994. Estonia were playing Croatia on the Sunday before Finland v Scotland on the Wednesday. They'd got the ferry over from Helsinki. Kenny never realised the two places were so close. They booked into the Hotel Viru, a complete monstrosity of an hotel which had been built by the Russians as their Intourist show hotel.

It had been a good game in a dilapidated stadium. Croatia had had several superstars playing for them and the fans had been granted free licence to roam everywhere. After the match somebody had complained that Prosinecki of Real Madrid was an ignorant bastard as he'd been sitting picking his nose as fans were wandering through the dressing room post match. The day was also memorable for Gus discovering cans of Estonian gin and bitter lemon. He had thought it would be like the old fashioned lager and lime he got when he was a kid, approximately 0.2 %. He hadn't realised it was the real deal with approximately four nips of gin a can.

After Gus had demolished three of the said cans in the

second half, he'd disappeared until the following morning when he had pitched up at the Viru to collect his gear. He had briefly mentioned a sauna, another two Scots guys, changing lots of money at 3am, three hookers, something about paying for it but not getting it and waking up fully clothed in the Hotel Suzi, five miles out of town. Kenny knew the full story would come out eventually and looked forward to that day with great interest, funnily enough.

At the time, he'd thought Tallinn was akin to a frontier town in the wild west but after the events of Riga, it would be like an eventide rest home. As he thought back, Jock Paisley's death still gnawed away at him. Hopefully, they'd be able to keep it out of the newspapers back home that he was with a hooker when it happened. Poor lassie. Knowing Jock, Kenny realised he wouldn't have paid until the services had been rendered, so there must have been a financial dimension to her state of distress.

He'd been pretty surprised at how quickly the police had appeared, then disappeared. They wrote it off straight away as dodgy electrics. They were confused as to why Jock was going into Kenny's room but they accepted his explanation with minimal fuss and had zoomed off as soon as.

The guy from the British Embassy was a different matter. The prick wouldn't have known a football if it had bounced off his head. When he looked at Jock Paisley he must just have seen pile of paperwork, no doubt to be completed in triplicate. To him they weren't British citizens, they were a temporary problem to be endured for as short a time as possible. If we could lose just a couple of passports, it would be a hindrance but no more than expected. If we decided not to decimate the city, even better. The repatriation of a body was another matter and it had got him out of his kip at 2 am on a Saturday morning. He was not a happy camper. Fortunately for Kenny, he had been able to summon an undertaker and get the body removed pretty quickly. Kenny wasn't sure if this was going down as "death by suspicious circumstances" or some such nonsense but death was fucking death so they had better get on with it.

Kenny gave a statement to the diplomat containing the best of his knowledge of what had happened but was inclined to leave the rest to Harry, Jock's pal who had been with the other hooker. It had not been a pleasant sight going up to Jock and Harry's room earlier on. The other old boy must have been keen to get on with it as he had left the door ajar. Kenny pushed it open and was greeted with the sight of a naked pneumatic Latvian blonde bouncing up and down on the face of a pensioner from Leith. From the contents of the glass on the bedside table at least he'd had the good grace to take his falsers out. No chance of pubes in the teeth there then.

To make matters worse, when the girl had eventually climbed off, her thighs had caused a vacuum in the old boy's ears and he couldn't hear a word until Kenny had encouraged him to swallow a couple of times. Kenny couldn't resist the temptation of giving him the glass of water to help him rinse his mouth out. The teeth went back in the mouth from the glass, but not quite in the manner Harry had hoped for, much to Kenny's amusement. He realised he had better screw the nut otherwise there would be a second corpse that night through choking on falsers.

When Harry got his teeth in the right way he was less than amused with Kenny and it had nothing to do with almost swallowing his false teeth.

"What the fuck are you up to ya daft cunt? I've only had twenty minutes worth and you come in here fucken ruinin it for me?"

"Harry calm down, I've got some bad news" said Kenny

"Bad news, you're the fucken bad news. Its taken me twenty minutes to get this fucking hard and now you've fucken ruined it"

Kenny now realised how distracted he had been by the hooker's activities and he looked down at an elderly but impressive hard on which did not exactly appear to be in the first stages of collapsing.

"It's Jock, I'm sorry Harry but there's been an accident and he's been electrocuted to death." Kenny was trying to find a bit of gravitas from somewhere. It was bad enough telling somebody their friend of forty years was dead but saying it to a pensioner who was standing in front of him, completely naked, with a stiffy you could balance a pint on was not exactly how he had imagined breaking the news.

"Get tae fuck! Are you on the wind up ya mad bastard?" shouted Harry

"No, there's no wind up. Go down to room 11. There's a few people that want to speak to you. You'll need to formally identify the body."

Every part of Harry had crumpled at the seriousness in Kenny's tone. In this case every part really meant every part and Kenny had been relieved to be no longer staring down the barrel of an angry Scottish cock. What a bloody night.

The bus continued on through the Estionian plains. More flat, empty fields, stretching out to a bleak grey horizon. In the depths of such boredom, it was hard to remember there actually had been a game in Riga. A fantastic 2-0 victory in which a couple of remarkable things had happened. Firstly, Scotland scored from what looked like a rehearsed free kick routine. Usually, it looked as if they had practised the free kicks with some circus clowns the element of slapstick was so high. The second remarkable thing was Darren Jackson scoring. Not only had he scored, but it was a tasty goal, involving a decent run into the area, before putting it past the keeper with no little skill.

The gaining of three points had been somewhat soured by the state of the stadium. The only gents was a passable copy of a trench at the Somme with a two inch coating of lime. It would appear that the Latvian idea of toilet cleaning was to cover everything in lime, which left you gagging for fresh air once you were out. Some guys had just gone behind the stand and had been having a quiet pee when the Riga police had appeared. Immediately, they began fining people on the spot. No paperwork involved, so he guessed all the fines had gone straight in the back pocket. One guy had been done for 20 lats, which equated to 20 quid. Kenny had been done for a fiver himself but the biggest laugh had been Gus maintaining he had no money on him. The cries of "Ahm fucking skint man. Your dodgy hookers have taken it off me. Go and arrest that tall blonde in Ronnie Whelans. She's got all my dosh. Ahm brassic lint. This is police harassment. 10 lats for a piss? How much would ye be wanting for a shite?" had echoed round the stadium just as the teams were coming out for the second half. Gus had missed Darren Jackson scoring the second goal but felt it was a small price to pay compared to, as he'd put it, "20 pound for a slash, get that tae fuck man." Bizarrely, the floodlights were the strongest Kenny had ever seen for a stadium that size. It was like something from the film Close Encounters of the Third Kind, if you looked directly at them.

They'd gone back up for the Under 21 game the next day. The stadium looked even worse in bright sunshine. They could see the covered terracing they had stood in the night before was a death trap with crumbling steps and poorly maintained crush barriers. On the opposite side of the ground, the windows of the "executive boxes" had all been put in, some journos were sitting at a table in one box, staring out at the U21 match through an open space. "Wouldnae mind the Everest franchise for this place" had been Gus's only comment. He'd taken the news of Jock Paisley's death badly as he was a good friend from way back.

This had detracted from Gus's earlier activities on the night of Jock Paisley's death. Gus had left the pub with Greta, as the girl was called, and a couple of other guys. They had gone back to a room in some hotel and proceeded to have what Gus described as the best group sex experience of his life. Kenny thought it was probably the only group sex experience he'd had in his life but didn't like to point that out. The night had threatened to go horribly wrong at one stage when, in a fit of extremely unbridled passion, Gus had moved round to kiss the girl on the lips, and had instead kissed big Hughie's cock as he was putting it into Greta's mouth. A nasty scene had been avoided only by Greta insisting it was a night for love not war and they were all friends. Hughie had taken a few minutes to recover his compusure and another five minutes to recover his erection. Gus had washed his mouth out with vanilla vodka, muttering about not knowing where people had been putting certain parts of their anatomy. For once Gus had taken his camera out with him and promised to show Kenny all the gory details once they got to Tallinn and he could get the film developed.

"Ah'm tellin ye man, the karma fucken sutra's got nothing on these photos. These are quantruple X never mind triple X. Yes, indeed, what a fuckin night, like. And to think people keep saying to me "Why are you wastin your time followin Scotland abroad?" How little they know man, how little they know. The third time ah came you couldnae have filled a teaspoon wi it, like but was ah complainin? Not on your nelly. One of the boys was keen on getting her to come up to Tallin wi us but she had to stay behind to wait for her boyfriend coming back. He's a long distance lorry driver. Bet he's never gone long distance wi his burd the way we did. Put a few miles on the cock that night did, that's for sure."

It had given Kenny an embarrassing amount of pleasure watching Gus's ecstasy turn to severe depression when he found out about Jock Paisley. Gus had really got to know Jock in Israel in 1981 when Dalglish got the winner in 1-0 world cup qualifier. At the time it had been mental, they'd got to know an Israeli bar owner who couldn't do enough for the troops. He even cashed Bank of Scotland cheques in sterling without any cards or guarantees. He'd had a private party before the game in his flat and the hospitality was unbelievable. What sealed Gus and Jock was a knife fight outside a nightclub in Jaffa the night before the game. Gus had been close to getting involved but Jock had wisely pulled him away to save Gus from further adventure, if not a trip to a Tel Aviv hospital's A + E.

This scenery just didn't get any better. More bloody trees. There was little or no traffic on the road. Another flat bit of land then more bloody trees. Any advertising hoarding was either boringly familiar, in that it was western, or it was totally unintelligible as it was written in Estonian. To be honest, there more going on inside the bus than outside due to the "interesting" characters on board. Kenny had had to ask one of the original Nottingham sixteen to sit down and stop singing. He was well into some song about his "rag a bag, shag a bag mother in law" when one of the girls had objected. Fair play to her but the miner had looked most put out. Gus had seen an opportunity and had gone up to offer her his support, saying there was no need for that kind of language from the guy and if he hadn't shut up he'd have gladly the decked the cunt for her. She thanked him kindly and then went back to the arms of her boyfriend who was doing a very good impression, at that point in time, of a man trying to make himself invisible. How long would this bloody bus take? The price of flights direct to Tallinn had been crazy but they were now looking cheap at half the price. 20/20 hindsight strikes again thought Kenny.

"Anybody see the bright lights of Tallinn?" asked Dominic.

"Don't worry, you'll smell this place before you see it," said Kenny

"That bad?"

"No as bad as Riga really but once you're in the Baltics and the smell of dill and cheap diesel hits your nostrils, you cannae get rid of it until you've been back in Scotland for three weeks. Ask sleeping beauty about dill, he just cannae get enough of the stuff".

Having had his advances spurned, Gus had crashed out. Dominic knew better than when to push it but did see the chance for a good photo opportunity. "You still got that banana from breakfast" he asked Kenny.

"Aye, it's around here somewhere. Don't tell me you're hungry?

"No, have you seen the way the wee man is sleeping?" Dominic pointed across the aisle to where Gus was draped across a double seat fast asleep. His head was leaning slightly over the seat edge onto the aisle and his mouth was wide open."

Dominic told Kenny to get the banana out, unzip his fly and then place the piece of fruit in his jeans so that it looked like his dick was hanging out. He then told him to stand with the piece of fruit dangling over Gus's mouth. Kenny achieved this with a little bit of difficulty as he didn't want to wake up Gus. Dominic had his camera ready and was waiting for the flash to come on. The rest of the bus had become aware of what was going on and Kenny was being encouraged to see how far he could put his fruit into Gus's mouth without the wee man waking up. He'd got it a good two inches in when the bus hit a pothole and Kenny's groin was thrust into Gus's face.

"wharefaaak" came the muffled shout from Gus. The rest of the bus howled with laughter as Gus tried to remove Kenny from his face whilst not choking on the banana. He had bitten right through the yellow fruit with the shock of what happened. He finally managed to sit up and spat out two inches of banana.

"You cunt" he cried "what the fuck did ye think ye were up tae? Ah've already had the misfortune to kiss one cock this trip and now ye're trying tae choke me tae death wi' a banana."

Kenny had hit his head on the luggage rack when the bus hit the pothole so was slightly dazed.

"What about my banana, wee man. I was going to have that for my tea! Did you get it?" he asked Dominic.

"I definitely got the point of entry, so congratulations, Gus.

With your eyes closed wee man it looked like you were in a euphoric state, just about to lovingly take Kenny's top banana in your warm and moist mouth. Ever ready to caress it to death with your strong darting tongue"

"Darting tongue, ah'll give you a darting boot up the arse Fraser. Ah knew a miserable fuck like you would be behind such a cruel stunt. Wait a minute, who the fuck was that? Was that you Bradley or have we just driven past a pig farm? Talk about silent but violent."

Kenny Bradley owned up to dropping a fart that smelt like something created in the depths of Porton Down chemical weapon research centre. Even Dominic Fraser was affected by it. "Jeezo Kenny. That's caught right at the back of ma throat. What you been eating to bring that on?"

"Nothing really, its just this gassy Baltic lager that makes me fart."

"Gassy lager? Anything makes you drop minging farts so for fucks sake don't blame it on the bevvy" erupted Gus. By this stage the last remnants of the fart were affecting the others seated around them. Kenny normally managed to absolve himself from blame by farting then immediately blaming some innocent party close at hand. This time the amusement of seeing Gus choke on a banana had clearly thrown him.

At this point everyone on the bus perked up as they realised they were finally coming into Tallinn. The street lighting was not the best but it was like the Blackpool illuminations compared to Riga. The city looked very quiet with a little traffic but few people on the streets. Brian came up to Kenny and told him they would be dropping off centrally first and then the bus would take Kenny, Gus and Dominic out to the Hotel Sport.

"What's the plans for tonight Brian?" asked Gus.

"Well its Tallinn so anything could happen but I guess we'll be looking for that bar owned by the Scots guy, is it the Nimita?"

"What kind of name is that for a bar?" asked Gus "be better off with no name than that crap".

Chapter 9

The Tallinn Job

KENNY AND GUS signed in at the Hotel Sport. It was a bit out of Tallinn but it was on the seafront. It had been built for the Moscow Olympics in 1980 to accommodate the sailing teams. The small matter of Moscow being 19 hours away by train hadn't seemed to bother the IOC, funnily enough, and for the Scotland fans, it was a good hotel at a good price. One of the biggest plusses was that it was not the Viru. When Kenny signed in, there was a brief confab between the receptionists and one of them eventually approached him and said "There is message for you". Kenny took the piece of hotel stationery and realised the holiday was over. The writing said "Scandic Palace Hotel, 9am". He didn't understand but he recognised the handwriting. Michael "Harold" MacMillan, his father in law was in town and requested his attendance. He knew he had to face the music with regard to Harold sometime but about what he had no idea. He had thought of phoning Alison to find out if she knew what was going on but then realised the less she knew the better.

"Oh well, there goes the party" he said to Gus.

"What do you mean? We've only just arrived, the party starts now. As Russ Abbott used to say "I love a little party atmosphere" and this town is party town," said Gus who had brightened up considerably since the incident with the banana.

"Aye well, maybe for you but I'm off to my bed. I've been summonsed to a meeting with Harold tomorrow at 9 am so I had better have my wits about me. Anyway I'm shagged out after that bus trip. Who would think sitting on your arse all day could be so tiring? It must be like working for a finance industry union."

At the mention of Michael MacMillan's nickname, Gus had started on his Albert Steptoe impression shouting "Harolld!!! Harolld!!! " at the top of his voice. He'd once been caught doing this by one of Harold's boys and was informed that if he didn't shut up, he would become a rag and bone man, as that was all that would be left of him, rags and bones. He had pulled up at the mention of the union and looked a little put out.

"There's no need for that. We work relentlessly for our members and no sacrifice is too great."

"What like leaving the pub on a Friday afternoon to do some work?"

"Ye're a bitter man Bradley, very bitter man to bring up work at this stage in the holiday," said Gus, a peeved tone to his voice.

"Aye well, you go on and enjoy yourself wee man. I am going to try and work out what the main man wants."And please, no dodgy hookers at 3 am, eh?"

Kenny went up to the room with the bags. He was pleasantly

surprised by the quality of the room and immediately did what any self respecting football fan does, checked to see what channel the porn was on. Things definitely seemed to be changing in Tallinn. Even on tonight's brief drive into the city centre, he got the impression a lot had changed in the two years since he was last here. Some wag on the bus had been going on about the Baltic tiger economy. He'd said the place was ripe for development and all the Baltic nations wanted to forge stronger links with the west. He even reckoned the three states, Estonia, Latvia and Lithuania would be in the EEC in the next decade. They might even try to get into NATO. Gus who had been sleeping up until the last bit of conversation blew the guys arguments to bits by asking if NATO was a nightclub in Tallinn.

Kenny unpacked and decided to have a shower before going to bed. The warm water acted as a reviver, so much so that he was tempted to jump in a taxi and head into town. He then put such thoughts to the back of his mind and tried to concentrate on what Harold could want with him. As he towelled himself off he gave up as he realised Sigmund Freud couldn't work out the goings on in Harold's mind, never mind a Glasgow cabbie. Looks like it will just have to wait until the morning, thought Kenny as he climbed between the sheets.

* * * * *

As Kenny was getting into bed, across town Atholl had just woken up. Since he'd arrived on the Saturday his time had passed in a blur of prostitutes, alcohol and cocaine. After checking in, he had gone down to the bar in the Hotel Viru and two hours later found himself in a a "menage a trios" with

127

two leggy Estonian blondes in the sauna of the Hotel Suzi. The hotel was set in a large Russian built housing estate on the outskirts of Tallinn and had been highly recommended by the barman in the Hotel Viru bar. The past couple of days had been a self indugent sexual blur but he had calmed things down and was getting up to go hunting not shagging. Atholl had realised with the bulk of the fans not coming up until the Monday he could afford to pass his time in some hedonistic pursuits as all he could do was wait for Kenny to come to him, once the games in Riga were passed. He showered and got dressed, then headed down to reception.

A group of fans were just checking in but he didn't recognise any of them and they paid him no attention as they were trying, with little success, to get an old communist era receptionist to check them in as quickly as possible. Atholl felt a twinge of sympathy for their plight. When he'd turned up without a reservation the two old biddies behind reception had gone into virtual meltdown over his simple request for a room for five nights. He left the hotel and crossed the road, heading up to the old town gate. He was going to stroll up to the town square and take it from there. He's asked around his various female companions over the last couple of days and they had told him there were many Scotland fans who were spending their money heavily on them. They had reeled off a list of bars and he thought he would trawl the bars until he found someone who might know where Kenny Bradley was staying. He didn't have long to wait.

He pushed open the door of the Hell Hunt and walked into Gus McSween who was carrying three pints of Guinness in his hands. " For fuck's sake man, watch where you're, Andy

Muir! How's it gaun? Gus' face lit up like the Riga floodlights when he realised it could be a night's drinking on somebody else's tab.

"Eh, fine, yourself?" asked Andy.

"Aye, no too bad as it happens. Flying solo like but it shouldnae be a problem. Kenny's a great guy but he can be a fourteen stone handicap when yir chasin fanny, like."

"Really, where is he then?"

"Tucked up in bed at the Hotel Sport if you're askin. He's got an important meeting the morn's morning,like."

"Who can he have an important meeting with in Tallinn?" thought Andy. He was just about to enquire further when he was bumped from behind. "C'mon Andy, this place is mobbed and there's too many Braveheart boys in kilts. We've nae chance here. We need to git in somewhere quieter wi local talent. "

Gus was pressed into Andy's face breathing Guinness and vodka fumes directly up his nose.

"Where are ye staying Andy?" enquired Gus as they squirmed into a bit of space and Gus handed out the pints to the two guys he was with, one of whom was a bemused looking Dominic Fraser.

"I'm in the Viru" replied Andy.

"Oh for fucks sake man, that monstrosity of an Eastern European tart's boudoir? What possessed ye to go there?"

"Eh, girl in the office booked it" muttered Andy, " you know how it is, some young sloaney type with her head up her arse books the first thing in the guidebook"

"Oh aye. Ah have the same problem aw the time wi ma job travellin round Fife. Ye jist can't get the staff," said Gus, a wry smile on his lips. He finished his Guinness in a long swallow, wiped his mouth with the back of his hand, burped and turned to Andy.

"C'mon, lets find some fanny."

* * * * *

The following morning Kenny sat in the taxi en route to the Scandic Palace. What passed for a morning rush hour in Tallinn consisted of numerous Coca Cola lorries clogging up a main road. "So things don't go better with Coke " after all thought Kenny. He'd had a good night's sleep, considering how Gus's arrival at 4 am had woken him up. Fortunately for Kenny, as requested, Gus had returned on his own. He'd been gibbering on about a beauty contest in a nightclub that was won by a Finnish girl whipping off her T-shirt in the final decider to reveal a pair of tits you could land a helicopter on. She'd won a weekend trip for two people to Edinburgh. What tickled Gus was that he knew that her boyfriend was Scottish. The laugh was that they actually lived in Edinburgh so there was fuck all point in them getting a holiday. "Some pair, mind you" were his last words before falling into the land of nod and Kenny didn't think he was talking boyfriend/girlfriend. The taxi took him past a well known Tallinn landmark, the Kik in de Kok. Excellent, Kenny thought to himself, the Kik in the Kok en route to a kick in the balls. Just what the fuck did Harold want with him?

As the taxi drew up he could see Harold looking out from a window in the coffee lounge next to the hotel reception. He looked alone but Kenny had no doubt his minders wouldn't be far away, Harold's personal assistants or in more straightforward terms scary, brutal, malicious, evil, large bodyguard bastards.

Kenny walked through reception to the table where Harold was sitting looking at a local paper.

"Didn't realise you were fluent in Estonian, Harold" said Kenny, sitting down in a chair opposite and wondering where the twins were as Harold looked completely alone.

Harold looked up and his face cracked a tight smile.

"There's a lot ye don't know about me Kenny but it's probably fur the best. Fur you that is. How's the trip so far? How many years ye taken off yer liver this time?" He put down his paper and appeared to be preparing himself for something. "You know I just drink to be sociable, Harold. Lets cut to the chase, what do you want to see me about?" Kenny had decided he was going to take the initiative in this meeting, what was it the Americans called it, "playing hard ball". That was it, he would be driving this conversation the way he drove his taxi.

Harold sighed and stroked his moustache. "Ah appreciate yer candour Kenny. Ah know ye're a busy man, the pubs'll be open in half an hour so ah'll keep it brief. Ye're a bright boy but a waster. Ye know ah don't like ye and but for the fact ah would never deny Alison anythin, the two of ye would never have got the gither let alone get married. However, once in a while ah get soft hearted and she knows right when to take advantage. A bit like her mother, God rest her soul."

This was not what Kenny had expected. A wee crack appeared in his hard balls. The caring sharing side to Harold MacMillan was even worse than the dark side. It would bring tears to a glass eye if he continued at this rate.

"But ah digress. Ah want to tell ye a story as Max Bygraves used to say. Ye remember Brian MacDowall don't ye? Ye met him briefly at Pollok Golf Club a few months ago."

"Oh aye, the bloke in the golf club bar" replied Kenny, not quite sure where this conversation was going and wondering how he was going to drive the conversation like his cab when he didn't know the direction it was taking, never mind the final destination.

Kenny thought hard and remembered a fleeting introduction to the guy in the clubhouse. He also remembered him calling his father in law by his nickname. A significant moment he remembered.

"Brian used to be a DS wi the Strathclyde Polis but somebody, who, ah should add, is no longer wi us, saw fit to grass up Brian for takin consultancy fees, as ye might call them, from ma company. Now Brian had been smart, nae flash car, nae exotic holidays or anything else drawin attention to his extra curricular income and he had done me a good turn or two. When the force found oot about oor, how shall ah put it, business relationship, he was offered the chance to resign or face the consequences. As ah said, Brian wasnae daft so he came to me and offered me a share in a private detective agency he was planning tae set up. Nice idea and a chance for me to make sure he didnae get humpty and go back to his old employers wi tales o where the bodies were buried, if ye catch my drift. The agency did well and it soon became part of a national network throughout the UK. Amazin' the number of bent coppers that decide tae continue in private law enforcement once their public service days are done or, tae be more accurate, they've been caught wi their hands in the till.

"What the fuck does this all have to do with me?" asked Kenny.

"Patience, Kenny, patience" replied Harold a frustrated look on his face.

He resumed his story. "So one day Brian gets this call fae London. A background job fur a client doon there. The usual stuff, personal history and some photos of the individual's current coupon. The name rings a very large bell with Brian. It turns into fire alarm style ringin when the individual's details get revealed tae me. Want tae know the name o the surveillance target?"

"I'm like a genetically modified mouse," said Kenny

"Whit?" said a bemused looking Harold

"All ears."

"Ok, smart bastard, listen to this. The name o the individual was Kenneth Joseph Bradley."

"No way." A slight chill played around Kenny's ears. It felt like someone had just opened a window behind him but he didn' turn round as he knew what was causing the sensation.

"Sorry but its you. Brian came tae me straight away and explained what the situation was. In fact, we were talking about it that day at the golf club. He'd tried to stall them initially, givin' oot a minimal amount o' detail. Sadly the client wanted mair personal background so he had to tell him more about you. Ah have tae admit ah was interested, no, that's no the word, intrigued aboot why anybody in the smoke would want tae know about ye? Brian was able to find out a couple of bits of info about the client so, out of pure curiousity, ah had this guy followed, did a bit of digging and got a few souvenir photos, just for a wee keepsake. Ah have them wi me now but before ah show them to ye, all ah want from ye Kenny is the truth. Ah need to know the reason why ye think anybody would be hirin' people to follow ye and look intae yer background. Ah knew it wasnae the polis as they wouldnae need to do this privately.

The next thing ahm thinkin o' is a jealous husband but that doesnae wash as who do you know in London? No cunt. All the time ahm gettin curiouser and curiouser. It's probably one of the reasons ahm here today. Rubbish disposal is a lot easier in these ex commy countries than it is at home. Or so ahm told."

Kenny suddenly felt even more uncomfortable. He had been amazed to find out he was being investigated. As if that wasn't bad enough, he knew if he didn't come up with a reasonable version of events in the next 10 seconds he would be swimming in the Baltic with concrete flippers.

"Harold, I don't know what to say." He managed to speak through lips which had gone curiously dry, his hard balls being shattered to dust a long time ago.

"Good, that's what ah wanted to hear because ah've even more to tell you," was the reply. Harold was smiling. Harold smiling was not good. Harold smiled rarely and only when he knew he was in a position to make someone suffer. This was not good, most definitely not good. On a not good scale of 1 to 10 it was a 39.

Harold reached under the table and pulled an A4 envelope out of his travel bag. He pulled three black and white photos out of the envelope and slid them across the table.

"Hae a look. Recognise the guy?"

"Aye, its Andy Muir, a posh Scot journo. He's appeared on the scene at the last couple of away trips" said Kenny.

He was looking down at a black and white photo of Andy Muir getting out of a very expensive looking sports car. It was parked in front of what looked like an office block. The second photo showed him emerging from what he'd sometimes heard referred to as a mews terrace house. The final photo showed him sitting in a crowd of Scotland fans in what appeared to be an airport lounge. Gus was there and Donny and then Kenny saw the image of himself, sitting just to the right of Gus.

"What the fuck is all this about?" said Kenny, an angry tone coming into his voice.

"Ahm not certain Kenny but a wee bit o' diggin has uncovered some rather unpleasant facts about our mystery man. Sorry, ex mystery man, Andy Muir. Ye've triggered the interest o a nasty wee piece of shite there Kenny. His real name is Atholl McClackit. He's a posh Scot like you say. Eton, Oxford and then quite interestingly, military intelligence. One o' Brian's guys is ex army and went back tae a couple o' his ex colleagues to see what they could tell him about the bold Atholl. The mention of his name resulted in a dead tone comin from the earpiece of the phone and funnily enough, they're still no returnin' his calls. Now where in the last 25 years has military intelligence been workin its proverbial nuts aff?"

"Luxemburg? Greenland? Northern Ireland?" Kenny was trying to buy a bit of time by cracking a few jokes. The direction the conversation had taken had his mind racing and his sphincter twitching.

"Well done, Kenny more to ye than just good looks. Ah had to dig a bit harder for the next information and it didn't come cheap but by this time ah was hooked. The Monarch of the Glen after my son in law? What's the silly prick done to deserve this?" Harold realigned himself in the chair. Kenny could see he was beginning to enjoy this wee chat.

"Anyway, after a wee bit stronger prying with the military it would appear Atholl was the brightest star for the army in the six counties for a good few years." Harold continued. " He had a nice wee network of informants from both sides helpin the army land a couple o' big munition hauls and allowin them to keep the tin lid on things in areas where the natives were getting restless."

Harold stopped talking to take a sip of his coffee.

"Funnily enough, his father had done exactly the same with the Mau Mau in Kenya in the 1950's. Well, that was until Atholl's star burnt out. His boss received an unusual request one day. A request for a meetin signed by the joint chiefs of staff of the IRA and the executive council of the UDA. Amazingly, they had a complaint. And dae ye know what the complaint was?

"Go on" murmured Kenny who was starting to lose his grip on reality.

"Atholl was costin them too much in terms of manpower and money."

"What?"

"Aye, ye can have too much o' a good thing. Wee Atholl was judge, jury and executioner in certain parts of Ulster. Catholic or Protestant, IRA, UDA, UVF, VHF. Everybody was fair game if they got in his way or didnae pay the protection money on time. Nobody could catch him as they didnae know what he looked like and the army gave him free rein. He made the SAS look like the Boys Brigade. Ah don't know how they managed to stop him but he was eventually brought under control and given a very honourable discharge."

"You seem to know an awful lot about his guy considering the ex army guys didn't want to talk about him" said Kenny.

"Kenny, for all ma faults, ye know I'm not bothered about religion. In the 70's in Glasgow ye had to be a bit nimble on your feet with these characters in Ulster. There was a lot of money to be made and ye had to have an open mind. Business is business. Unfortunately wi Alison's mother ah wasnae quite nimble enough".

Kenny remembered Alison had only ever once dropped her guard about her dad. She had told him her mother was killed by a car bomb in 1972. It had been meant for her dad but her mother had taken his car early one Sunday morning to get fresh rolls and was blown to smithereens.

"As ever, I don't have a clue what you are talking about Harold." said Kenny whose levels of concern about his personal well being were going right off the scale.

"Look, ah had tae deal with a variety of people who didnae all have the same viewpoint regardin Northern Ireland. That's all ah can say. Ah still have some contacts there and they could provide me with the information on your wee pal Atholl or Andy Muir as ah believe he's now called. The army wish the guy had never been born but they have to look after their own. He did everythin they needed or wanted done if the boys of the old brigade are to be believed."

Kenny was stunned. "I still don't understand how you've found all this out about the guy. I thought he was a journo called Andy Muir. If he was taking out half the IRA and the UDA, I think they might be a wee bit interested on what he was up to these days and they might have looked for him already" he remarked in a urgent voice.

"Keep it down Kenny, we don't want to attract too much attention to ourselves." said Harold. "These guys were so happy to see the back of wee Atholl they agreed not to take it any further. When Brian was looking into Andy Muir there was a lot o loose ends. No school records, gaps in employment history aw that sort of thing. It was only when he looked into things like whose name his house was in and other areas it became apparent Andy Muir didnae exist, but a certain Atholl McClackit did. Ahve also got a wee laddie who's a bit of a computer whizz. He came in to one the massage parlours near the uni the first day he got his student grant. Blew the load in a week on blow jobs and tit fucks. He approached Willie the manager wi a proposition as he had no money but he could order white goods over something called the internet using fake credit cards. Could we accept them as payment? You know, a fridge for a fuck sort o thing. Talk about the appliance of science. Well, when ah heard about his skills ah got him on a retainer. He's managed tae hack, ah think that's the word, into the personnel records of the company "Andy Muir" works for and it's all there. The company is an international security consultancy and Atholl McClackit is their risk assessor. It's owned by some ex-army contact o' his and that's where we got his personal details."

"But what's all this got to do with me?" said Kenny who felt close to a nervous breakdown.

Harold paused to take another sip of his coffee. Kenny's head was nipping, Mau Mau, IRA, UDA, somebody actually with a first name of Atholl, it was all getting too much for him.

"Ah don't know Kenny, ye'd have to ask him yoursel but I wouldn't advise gettin that close to him'" replied Harold. Harold looked at Kenny and wondered if he'd told him too much. He was concerned for a variety of reasons and with all he had planned, this was one distraction he did not need, not now at such a crucial time with regards the wee job planned for tomorrow. He didn't know what Kenny had done to rattle this boy's cage but he knew one thing. From what he'd seen, Atholl was one wee fucker you didn't want to mess with and, unfortunately for him, his chump of a son in law had managed to do just that.

"Anyway, gettin back to the here and now, the thing is, ah've a wee job going on tomorrow and ah need a bit of a diversion about 3 pm. We're thinkin o' gettin the game moved from an evening' kick off to an afternoon KO. Ma pal here has contacts and they've brought in some dodgy floodlights for the game. Apparently the stadiums a shitehole and they've no permanent floodlights. The Estonian Football Association's got these stage lights in but we've made sure they're about as powerful as a 2 years old fart. To put the cherry on it ah've a couple of sets of negatives of members of the association committee gettin up to things in one of my saunas that their wive's might be interested in. So ah will be having a word and tellin them to propose to the high heid yin fae the UEFA or FIFA the lights are fucked and we'll get an afternoon KO. Job done, eh? What ah need you to do is to go there this afternoon and make sure for me they are as bad as the boy says. Ye know more about the game than any o these cunts so ah just need a second opinion. Ok?"

Kenny's head was spinning. Get a game moved? Get a world cup qualifier moved as a diversion to a crime? Its madness, complete and utter madness.

"Aye, ok Harold. No problem," he replied.

Chapter 10

Light Fantastic

KENNY AND DOMINIC were sitting round a table in the Nimita bar with some other fans talking about the Under 21 game which was going to kick off in a couple of hours. Earlier on they had been to a memorial service for those who died when the SS Estonia sank in the Baltic Sea, two years before. A few fans had been on the boat itself, the week before it sank, so it definitely was a case of there but for the grace of God go I.

It had been a grey old morning in Tallinn with a bit of a chill in the air. There had been a get together outside the town hall first thing where the Scotland fans who had been able to surface had met the mayor to express their consolations. There had been a few murmurs of discontent when a well known face in the TA had handed over a City of Glasgow plaque and insinuated it was only right and proper as most of the fans were from Glasgow. They'd then walked along the main drag near the old town wall to the memorial site. Kenny had had the misfortune to fall into stride with the attache from the British Embassy whose conversation had been nearly as miserable as the weather. It didn't help that the diplomat's presence reminded Kenny of the last time he had met a member of Her Majesty's Diplomatic Corps, just a few days earlier in Riga.

At the ceremony itself, the lament played by the piper had made Kenny feel even more depressed, especially as the piping coincided with the start of a light drizzle. It was all a bit much, coming on top of his earlier conversation with Harold. He'd also had a bit of trouble coming to terms with the monument itself which looked like two pieces of liquorice, one of which was coming out of the ground in a bend and the other was sticking out of the top of a raised banking. One guy was astute enough to get the symbolism. It was, he thought, meant to represent a wave crashing into the prow of a boat. Kenny could see it now but the subtlety of the monument had initially been lost on him. Gus had left part way through the ceremony as he couldn't take it. Drizzle probably making him homesick for Dumfries thought Kenny.

Gus walked into the Nimita bar, his face tripping him. As he approached the table where they were sitting, he exploded into yet another rant , "Ahve had it with this place man. The Russians might have gone but it's still a police state, like. The freedom of the individual counts for nothin here. Ah thought they had an open mind, boundaries that previously existed were being taken down and replaced with a new open minded view on life, like. This is the most blinkered shower of cunts ah have ever come across. If this is the free world, they can fucken keep it. Ah cannae wait tae get back to the west where life is for the livin and you're not restricted by petty rules and bureaucracy."

"What's gone wrong now?" Kenny asked Gus, wondering what could have got him going so badly.

"Ma photos that's what's gone, never mind gone wrong." replied Gus

"Why what's wrong with them? I thought you put them into that photo shop off the square to get developed?" Kenny could see the wee man was upset and he was trying his best to placate him.

"Ah did. The bird in the shop, who looked a right old witch, by the way, said they would be ready in an hour. Ah've been for a wee walk, had a freshener in the Hell Hunt and then went back to collect the photos, like."

"So, what's the problem?" enquired Dominic

"So, what's the problem?" Gus mimicked Dominic's voice in a sarcastic tone. "The problem is ah get the photos of our sex session in Riga and ah'm goin through them thinkin there's somethin missin here, like. Ah remembered it was 36 spool film that ah put in ok?. As ahm walkin down the road ah count the photos and there's only 14 of the bastarts. So ah go back tae the shop and point this out to the old cow. By the way, I'm 22 shots short here doll, whit's the jackanory like?"

"So what did she say? " asked Dominic

"Well the Wicked Witch of the north says "Yes, this film I remember. In Estonia, we not allowed print photos of more than two people in the sex."

"Ah said "more than two people in the sex, what are you on about?" "You, with two men and woman in the sex in photo" she replied. Then I realised the boy wi the camera had obviously got a bit creative while we were on the job, like, an put the lot of us in the photo, no just the odd shot o' me and Greta. Whit a nightmare, like.

"Fuck me, I never realised it was a wide angle lense on that camera. It would be a struggle to get her in one photo never mind the four of you" said Dominic. "Then again, I suppose it was an intimate wee pose."

"Shut it you, what does a virgin know about erotic art? So ahm in the shop and ah was a bit embarrassed as you can imagine so ah had to leg it but the more ah think about it, the angrier ah get like. Their ma photaes and ahm bein' persecuted by the petty rules which govern this country!"

"Have you thought about bribing her?" asked Kenny.

"What the fuck are you on about? Bribing her? To do what exactly?" erupted Gus. It had been a crap day so far and it didn't appear to be getting any better from where he was sitting.

"Well, you know that there is a low wage in Estonia compared to the west, you could go back and offer her some money to be a bit flexible with the rules. You were complaining we didn't offer a big enough bribe when we came through the border, now you're bottling it." said Kenny.

"There's a difference between a border guard and a lassie that works in a photo lab," replied Gus who nevertheless was considering it a serious option.

"What's the difference? They're both probably paid peanuts and in her case she might be able to do something on the side for you. Go back and explain those photos had sentimental value for you as it's the first time you've ever kissed a man's cock. I can't wait to tell Cammy you've gone bi"

"Do that and it will be the last thing you do, ya bastard. The idea of the bribe's a good one though. Where do you get those brains fae, Bradley? Good work. ahm away to have a word wi' her now. See youse cunts at the Under 21s."

Gus bounced out of the pub after they agreed to meet him at the U21 game.

"What we doing about getting to the game Kenny?" asked Dominic.

"Just cab it. Want to go now and see what's happening?" replied Kenny.

"At an Under 21 game? What the fuck ever happens at these games except a bunch of malnourished youngsters, the future of the Scottish game, I should add, get humped," was Dominic's reply.

Kenny laughed at the all too accurate description of the young Scotland team. "I'm going out anyway, I might have a word with Frances Fairweather when I'm out there, see how life's treating her."

"Ok I'll see you there. If you see her tell her I was asking for her. Tell her I'm looking for a big interview for the fanzine".

Kenny left the bar and turned right towards the taxi rank. He said hello to a couple of familiar faces en route and took the first taxi available. Hardly anybody was moving towards the ground yet as it was still an hour to kick off. If what Harold MacMillan had said was true, the whole thing was going to go tits up the following day and there was nothing he could do about it. He couldn't honestly believe Harold and his contacts would get the game moved, but if he could speak to Frances, he might be able to find out if she knew anything about the possibility of a rearrangement and where that would leave the fans. Frances Fairweather was in charge of the Scotland Supporters Club. What she knew about football you could write on the back of a stamp in capital letters but when it came to handling Scotland supporters she was in a class of her own. He'd never understood how she got into the job but whoever had appointed her had got extremely lucky. Maybe he should be picking the team.

As for his other problem, he didn't know what he was going to say to Andy or Atholl or whatever the fuck his name was when he saw him but he was sure he would think of something. Would he even be here? Kenny hadn't seen Atholl again in Riga so fuck knows where he was now. Better to start thinking abut the floodlights thought Kenny but his mind kept drifting back to the meeting with his father-in-law earlier on.

Towards the end of the conversation this morning, Harold had asked him how many Scotland fans died on trips. Kenny had known it to happen before but had no hard stats. Harold had then gone on to point out that in the last two away games, a fan had died on each trip. Weren't those stats a little higher than average? All this had started since Atholl had begun trailing Kenny Bradley. Kenny was getting a very uncomfortable feeling in his chest and realised he needed to do something to calm himself down and not create any greater panic than he had already created for himself. He then realised he was going to a Scotland Under 21 game so it was clear the only foreseeable emotion in the future was depression, especially if it had been as bad as the 0-0 draw in Riga.

His taxi pulled up at the entrance to Kadriorg Park and Kenny got out, trying to come to terms with the fact that within this public park was a ground that was capable of hosting an international football match. Aye right. He walked through a heavily wooded section of the park before arriving at the ground. The pitch had a couple of walls but was mainly surrounded by chain link fences. There was a small main stand but apart from that, the whole ground was open to the elements. He saw immediately what Harold had meant regarding the floodlights. The bottom light was barely four yards off the ground and there was hardly twenty feet between the bottom row of four and the top row. Whoever in the Estonian FA had gone for this option, as opposed to playing in daylight, had fucked up bigtime. He was wondering what to do next when he heard a female voice behind him say "Mr. Bradley, what a pleasure to see you. As ever, it is fantastic to know you have arrived in good time to get into the ground and find your seat before kick off". Kenny turned to see a slight woman in tan raincoat. Her blonde hair was immaculate and she wore a big smile on her face.

"Alright, Frances. How ye doing?" asked Kenny

"Very well Kenny, and yourself? Is young Mr McSween not with you today? enquired Frances.

"No, he's had a problem with getting some photos developed that he took in Riga. You should ask him about them when you see him, I'm sure he'll be glad to explain it to you. You might even be able to help him, given your expertise with a camera."

"I'll ignore that last remark" said Frances with a knowing look in her eye. Frances Fairweather was renowned amongst fans for being appalling at taking photos. A number of times fans had given her their camera to get a photo taken with a player only to see a collection of headless torsos or vast tracts of sky on display once the photos had been printed.

"So any new ice cream parlours in Tallinn?" asked Kenny. Along with her photographic ability, Frances was also noted for her sweet tooth and love of ice cream.

"Sadly not, but they have a new pastry chef in our hotel who makes the Estonian equivalent of caramel shortcake so there's been no withdrawal symptoms, so far. And what about you? How's the lovely Alison?"

"Aye great, no problem. I see they've done nothing to this

place since the last time I was here," said Kenny gazing around at what he thought was a disaster waiting to happen.

"No, they haven't done much to it have they? Its hard to believe this a ground that is fit to hold a World Cup qualifier," said Frances "but I am sure everything will be all right on the night"

"Are you absolutely certain about that?" Kenny was trying not to let his panic show, but it was a bit of a struggle.

"Why shouldn't it be?" enquired Frances. She could play the innocent very well when it suited her. Most of the time she took on a naïve outlook to save fans from themselves but Kenny knew beneath her, at times girlish demeanor, there was a razor sharp brain.

She was also aware of his family connections and whilst never being so crass as to ask what his wife did for a living, he was certain she knew all about the MacMillan dynasty. In fact she knew too much, as any fan would verify. Many fans had come away from a first meeting with her wondering how on earth she knew so much about them.

"Well, I was having a look at these floodlights before you turned up and they don't exactly look international class. You'd be struggling to light up a Subbuteo pitch with these." replied Kenny.

"Funny you should say that as one of our committee members has just said exactly the same thing.".

Kenny quickly turned to face Frances and she was giving him what could only be described as a funny look. Not funny ha ha but funny as in "If you know something and don't tell it to me, you bastard, I will make sure you never get a ticket for another Scotland game."

Kenny realised he had to get a grip, "Eh well, don't want to take up too much of your time Frances. I'm sure you've got a lot more meeting and greeting to do. Ah'll see you in the ground." said Kenny who started to walk backwards whilst saying his goodbyes.

"I'm sure you will Kenny, I'm sure you will," said Frances, the knowing look never leaving her eyes for a moment.

Kenny walked up to the ground and was directed into the ground by a couple of bored looking riot cops. You didn't actually have to pay to see the match as the fencing was, at best, inadequate. If you put up with looking through a chain link fence you could save a big 75p. Kenny was sure there would be a few who would do it as well.

He climbed up the steps to the area which was to the right of the main stand as you looked at the pitch. The word "main" could easily be substituted with "only". The teams were warming up. As usual, Kenny could barely identify three of the Under 21 team. If these were meant to be the prime of a nation's youth, Scotland was fucked big time. Small and slight was the most positive spin you could put on the appearance of most of them with their bleached skins, wasted shoulders and a smattering of acne thrown across half their faces. More like Junkie U21s than Scotland U21s thought Kenny. As the Scotland fans slowly drifted into the ground, Kenny was greeting a few familiar faces. A couple of guys appeared with local women in tow, including, a few rows down, a face Kenny hadn't seen for some time which belonged to Jamesie Cresswell.

"Jamesie, how's it going son? Long time no see, no since where? Moscow? Helsinki?" shouted Kenny.

Jamiesie looked up with a less than impressed expression.

"Alright Kenny how you doin? Aye, havnae seen ye since Moscow. I'll catch you later". He then turned back to his female companion and re started his conversation.

Kenny was a bit perplexed by this as he couldn't understand the cold shoulder treatment. He walked down the stand until he was in the same row as Jamesie and wandered up to him.

"You alright, Jamesie?" he enquired.

"Aye, brand new Kenny, its just ahm wi company and ah don't want her to feel neglected, ken". Jamesie was looking at him with a rather pleading look on his face. Kenny realised now would be a good time to do the decent thing and walk away so not cramp another fan's style. Then again, when did the decent thing and the Tartan Army ever walk had in hand so he ploughed on.

"No going to introduce me to your new friend then, Jamesie?" said Kenny, a broad grin on his face.

"Eh, oh aye, Kenny. Eh, this is eh, eh, Mingo" said Jamesie, who could not look Kenny in the face as he said the girl's name.

"Mingo!" said Kenny, managing to stifle a guffaw as he offered the girl his hand.

"Hi, nice to meet you" came a muted reply from the small Estonian blonde with a name no Scot would ever forget.

"Eh, ok, Jamesie, I'll just leave you to it" said Kenny.

As he turned to leave, Jamesie grabbed his arm and whispered in his ear "You mention her name to McSween and I'll never forgive you. That wee cunt finds out I'm wi a burd called Mingo, ah'll never hear the end of it. Ahm beggin ye"

"Aye, ok Jamesie, your secret is safe wi me" said Kenny and he walked back up the steep steps to where he was originally standing. Ten minutes later Dominic and Gus turned up and stood next to him.

"See Frances?" enquired Kenny.

"Aye ah did and if it hadnae been for the result ah had in the photo shop, courtesy of your good idea, like, ah would be well fucked off wi you at this moment in time, by the way" replied Gus.

"Whats wrong now? Did she ask about the hair transplant?" said Kenny

"No she didn't, smart bastart. She asked about my photos, like, what the problem was, were they o' Riga tourist sights and could she see them sometime as she hadn't got much o' a chance to see the city when she was there. You grassed me up to her, didn't you?"

"I merely pointed out you had a wee problem and she might be able to help," replied Kenny.

"Fuck off man, she knows as much about photography as ah do about nuclear fusion. But ah'll forgive ye as that's the sort of man ah am, like. Ah'm bigger than your petty vindictiveness"

"Aye but no much" interrupted Dominic.

"One more crack out of you, Fraser!"

"So what happened at the photo lab then?" enquired Kenny.

"As it happens the old McSween charm worked a treat, like. Ah went back in and told her ah'd forgotten to leave a tip for her. Ah said the quality of the photos that were developed was excellent and ah only wished we had somebody like her in Glasgow. We got chattin and the end result is ah've to meet her tomorrow at 3 pm. She'll do the photos herself tonight when the boss has gone and ah'm taking her out for a wee pre match meal, like. If it goes alright, she might come to the match wi' me and then we'll see where the night and the music take us. Bit of a result, eh?" Gus rubbed his hands together. His sense of expectation was off the sexual richter scale.

"Whatever happened to the Wicked Witch of the north bit?" asked Dominic trying to do a bit of a spoiler on Gus's joy.

"Well, maybe I was a wee bit hasty, like. If ye took the horn rimmed glasses off and she let her hair down, she would a be a real looker. What's that song "That Old Black Magic Cast a Spell on Me", aye the wee man might just be in love again, like"

"Aye if she's a real witch, maybe she can make that photo of you kissing Hughie's cock disappear." quipped Dominic

"See you, Fraser, you're getting right on ma tits. As if watching this heap of pre pubescent shite disgrace the jersey isnae bad enough, ah have to put up with your so called humour".

"Calm down for fucks sake, where's your famous Scottish sense of humour" said Kenny trying to cool the situation. "Try and concentrate on the game. Then again."

It had been a turgid first half and as the light began to fade it took little to deflect Kenny's attention from the game and onto the floodlights. They were struggling to see the far side of the pitch by the time the game ended and Kenny realised that blackmail or no blackmail, somebody somewhere could make a legitimate complaint and they would have a very good case for getting the game moved or, at worst, postponed. It really did not bear thinking about.

"Anybody up for shepherd's pie in the Hell Hunt" suggested Gus.

"I thought you hated dill and vowed never to eat anything

151

apart from McDonalds once you were here" Dominic retorted.

"Aye well, ah suppose ah can make an exception this time, like. That shepherd's pie o theirs is the "chiens ballons". You coming Kenny or you going to see Frances and leave me with this miserable cunt Fraser for company?" asked Gus.

"Aye, I'll see you in there. Just got a wee bit of business to sort out first" said Kenny as he wandered down the aisle to the front of the stand.

Kenny made his way out with the rest of the crowd. It was a muted scene as it had ended up a 1-0 victory for Scotland but the overall performance was poor, bordering on complete shite. You had to feel for Alex McLeish managing this lot. They had been gubbed 4-0 in Austria where it looked like 11 proles versus 11 specimens of the master race. You looked at the guys in the Scotland shirts and thought, Scottish football has no future, they would be better giving up now. However, the bigger picture could wait as he was more concerned with the "here and now" or to be more precise, the "here and tomorrow".

He found Frances dealing with a couple of irate fans who had bought tickets for the full game in a ticket shop in Tallinn and were complaining that the price charge to locals was a lot cheaper than the SFA's price for match tickets. Do these pricks never realise its not the SFA that set the price but the home team he wondered. He lingered on the fringes until he caught her eye. In a way only she had, Frances gave these guys a polite fuck off by asking them what their supporters club membership numbers were. This cut the legs from their argument as they were not members and could never have bought tickets from the association anyway. Ah, the lost Scottish art of complaining for the sake of complaining. Driving a taxi had exposed Kenny to more than a couple of these sorts, so Frances had his full sympathy.

Frances walked over to Kenny with a fierce look in her eye "Is there something you want to tell me?" she demanded.

"Nothing that I can say for sure but did you not think those floodlights looked a bit dodgy for a night game?"

"I hadn't thought about it. Surely they have been approved by FIFA as they've played night games here before."

"Yeah but at what time of the year? This is the land of the midnight sun and from what I can see at the moment, they're just not up to it."

They were now standing on the opposite side of the pitch from the main stand which was barely visible in the early evening Estonian gloom, even with the floodlights on.

"As I said before, is there something you want to tell me?" asked Frances.

At that moment the lights were turned off and the stadium fell under a blanket of darkness.

"What's that quote from the First World War?" asked Kenny. "The lights are going out all over Europe"

"We may not see them on again in our time" said Frances completing the quote.

"You said it," said Kenny.

Chapter 11

Pre Match Build Up

HAROLD MACMILLAN WAS nervous. He normally got nervous before a job, but this time he was in a foreign country relying on a guy he'd met on a golf course in the Caribbean. Not only that, they were depending on the moving of a World Cup qualifier kick off time to act as a distraction for the authorities. He couldn't believe it when the two prats from the International Committee said they had done it. It was only later, after he'd handed over the negatives, he'd established from Kenny it would have been called off anyway, the floodlights really were that bad. The relevant individuals would be contacted at a later date to be informed of his dissatisfaction regarding their claim on achieving what he's asked of them, when they had had hee haw to do with it, but that was for back in Scotland. The ongoing situation was another matter.

Harold and his Estonian partner had planned everything down to the last second when he'd brought up the issue of Atholl. His plan had not gone down well initially with the Estonians but he'd pointed out the benefits and they had calmed down. They had been planning to use contacts on the inside to help them pull the job off. What Harold proposed would allow them to take the heat off those inside, pointing the authorities in completely the wrong direction. As far as he could see it, which admittedly wasn't very far, given his false eye, it wasn't so much a win/win situation as a complete doing.

The boys were in their element. They had endured a bonding session with Leo's bodyguards in a local brothel and it was all brotherly love in the bodyguard world. "The team that drinks, shags and snorts coke together, wins together" could be a new motto above his desk at work. Just as long as it didn't affect their performance on the day, he didn't give a flying fuck. He wasn't sure how things would pan out with the local police after this but Leo seemed confident he could placate them, leaving Harold to make an easy exit. He had to admit this game turning up had been a stroke of luck. He had come in as a fan and could leave as a fan, or at least appear to. From what he'd seen the locals would be sad to see the Scots depart. He hadn't been on one of these sort of trips since a Wembley weekend in the early 1960's and he'd forgotten just how much money Scots were keen to throw about.

It had been an incredible sight at times Guys who, back in the wilds of Fife, would have cut off their right arm rather than pay for a cab were getting taxis willy nilly and, even more incredibly, they could be seen to be tipping. God knows how the Estonian men treated their women as some of these guys were getting laid on the offer of taking a local girl out for a meal.

He'd met one guy who worked in the council offices in Kilmarnock. The guy was called Brian and had stumbled into Harold in the hotel bar. The boys had offered to remove him from Harold's company but he'd calmed them down as the guy had been quite amusing. He'd admitted he was nothing, had a shite job in a shite place, as he so quaintly put it, but these trips allowed him to be somebody. He only went on the Eastern European trips because the bevvy was cheap and he felt like superman as he could afford to buy anything he wanted. He'd got to know a local burd and she was keen on coming over to see him, if he paid for her ticket. He was sure it wasnae a passport job as he knew the look of love when he saw it and she'd definitely got it when she looked at him. More likely when she looked at your wallet, thought Harold but good luck to her. Once she'd had a look at Cumnock she'd be on the first flight back to Tallinn. They say love is blind but no that blind.

Harold had pulled Kenny out of the swimming pool at the Hotel Sport earlier on that morning. They'd got the word from FIFA that the game was to be brought forward to 3pm which fitted perfectly with their plans. He had explained to Kenny what would happen, giving him the minimal amount of information. The less he knew the better for him. Harold didn't have any problem with what was going to happen to Atholl, he'd tried to kill a member of Harold's family and whilst there was once a time he might have encouraged him in his task, he'd come to see just how much Kenny meant to Alison. Christ, listen to me, I'm getting totally fucking sentimental ,thought Harold. Nothing like a wee job to put me back on the mean and callous track. He'd arranged for the boys to keep an eye on Kenny as he thought Atholl would be around somewhere and this time Atholl would maybe get more than he bargained for. He'd asked Leo to see if he could find an Andy Muir registered in any of the Tallinn hotels and, if he did, keep an eye on him.

* * * * *

Kenny had been amazed it had all come off. He didn't want to
know what Harold was up to but he knew it must be big for
him to come all the way here in person. A gesture of faith to the
Estonians? He lay floating in the pool considering what Harold
had told him half an hour ago. A dip first thing was the perfect
cure for a hangover and, after his night in Club Hollywood, he
was enjoying every minute of his pool time. He and Gus had
ended up in the nightclub after a couple of hours in the Nimita
after the U 21 game where they had been forced to suffer various
minor Scottish media celebrities belting out Beatles hits over
the PA system. The band in the nightclub had been little better.
Their stage wear was reminiscent of the Clash circa Combat
Rock but their music had barely moved past 1960. Kenny had
been highly amused to see a number of Scots get local girls up
to dance only to watch them lumber about, even worse than
they usually did, when they heard they would be dancing to
Estonians doing a cover version of "Blue Suede Shoes".

As he lay back in the refreshing waters, he realised he'd
better tell Gus about the KO time being moved. He wouldn't
be happy as it cut his pre match drinking down to three hours,
maybe less if he didn't get his arse into gear. He put on a robe
and wandered over to a house phone. After twenty rings he
heard a croaky voice go "Whit?"

"Its me, Kenny. Look, I know you won't believe this and I
am not winding you up. They've moved the kick off to 3pm.
The floodlights are sub standard and FIFA have told them to
move the game forward" said Kenny.

"Whit?" groaned Gus a bit more force creeping into his voice
this time.

"The game's kicking off at 3pm. Its 11.00 now so you'd better get your act together and have a shower and get the battledress on as the games's this afternoon, not this evening".

A quick "No problem" and the phone went dead. Christ, that was easy thought Kenny. He'd decided not to go back into the pool as knew this hotel had a big fuck off sauna somewhere. He was sure this would remove the last remnants of the hangover. He hung up his robe and wandered round the pool looking for the sauna. He finally found it at the far end and wandered in. It was blasting out steam full throttle in a large room with 12 plastic bucket seats around the edges of the room. Now this is what I call a sauna thought Kenny, no like some of those lukewarm garden sheds back home wi a bucket of fake coal in the corner. Kenny could only make out a couple of pairs of ankles which he presumed were male given their thickness, then again he'd seen a couple of Scottish girls here with their boyfriends earlier on so he thought he'd better keep his speedos on, just in case.

Pity nobody else was here for a wee chat but he wondered how long he would last it was so hot. One of the locals got up and started stretching a bit. He gave it a few arm swings and then walked out of the sauna and stepped straight in the plunge pool next to the sauna. Seems like a good plan thought Kenny and got up. At this point a shape appeared out of the mist and said, "Hello Kenny, fancy bumping into you here." It was Atholl.

Oh fuck thought Kenny. Before Kenny could say anything Atholl had his hands round Kenny's throat and was applying maximum pressure to his Adam's apple. Within seconds Kenny was seeing bright silver lights flashing through the steam of the sauna. Bastard he thought and tried to fight back, but it was useless. Too many lagers and too many curries had reduced him to a pathetic state. He really is trying to kill me thought Kenny but why? So many questions and no fucking answers. Kenny flailed his arms around but resistance was pointless. As the steam parted for a brief second, he glimpsed Atholl's face, pent up with anger. But why me thought Kenny as he started to black out. At that, the pressure was suddenly released and as he staggered back, he could make out Atholl falling to the ground through the steam. He looked up to see the boys looming large through the clouds.

"All right Kenny?" asked Alec, the friendlier of the two.

"Aye, aye, just about. Where have you been sittin?" spluttered Kenny as he tried to massage some feeling back into his throat.

"We were in the corner. Got a tip off fae Leo's minders this wee cunt was in the hotel and was watching you. We beetled over just in time, by the looks of things. Don't know what he would have done if you hadnae come in here but he's a game wee cunt. Had to hit him three times before he went down. Once on the napper and then once behind each knee. Most impressed but still, he went down."

"What are you going to do now?" asked Kenny.

"Don't worry, Kenny. Harold's got plans for this wee shite" said Tony the other "boy". He smiled which to Kenny was equally as uncomfortable as Harold smiling. He realised then that whatever happened to Atholl was going to be quite, no totally, unpleasant.

"Alright Tony, I'll get the laundry basket. If he comes round and tries anything just smack him again."

"No probs Alec. Want to disappear Kenny?" enquired Tony.

"Could be an idea. Thanks, that's one I owe you" said Kenny

as he stepped over Atholl and prepared to leave the sauna.

Tony was shaking his head in a bemused fashion. "One you owe us? Ha Ha. Did you hear that Alec? Robert de Niro here owes us. Aye right. Catch you later, Kenny. Now fuck off out of it, ya cunt".

That fucking Robert de Niro crack yet again. Alright, the bastard might have saved his life but ever since Tony had seen Taxi Driver he had been needling him, going on about when was Kenny going to get a mohican and asking how Cybil Shepherd was doing. Still what was he going to say in reply that wasn't going to get him killed. Thinking of that, what the fuck had he done to wind up this Andy or Atholl guy so much?

He quickly legged it out of the pool area and into the changing room. He had a quick shower and dried himself off. When he got back to the room, Gus was pulling on a Timberland boot and whistling.

"Whats up wi' you?" enquired Kenny.

"Dominic's just been on the phone. The Estonians are threatenin tae no turn up. It's an inter fucking national incident. We're going to be the centre of the known world this afternoon pal, you'd better believe it. And you know what really good thing is?"

"What's that?"

"We'll be there. What a game to be at. Ah'll tell be telling ma grandchildren about this one" said Gus who started whistling again to the tune of Oasis' "Champagne Supernova".

"What the fuck has "Champagne Supernova" got to do wi this state of affairs and when do you plan to have children never mind bloody grandchildren?" said Kenny.

"We'll be drinkin champagnski the night if they don't turn

up, won't we? If they bottle it, they've forfeited the game and we get the three points. What a double header this is, like, two clean sheets and six points. The Austrians and the Swedes will be spewing. Parlez vous francais, Kenny? Ya beauty, France 98 here we come. Grandchildren? Ye know ah've always wanted to have kids. How long have we known each other? Don't tell me you don't see me as a responsible parent?"

"I give up" said Kenny and lay down on his bed. "No game and now you're telling me you want to become a father. The world's gone mad."

"Come on you, pull yoursel the gither. Ah said we'd meet Dominic at half eleven in the lobby. We'll get a cab into town to make sure everybody else knows the score. How did you find out anyway?" asked Gus.

"I was in the pool and Harold came and told me the game had been moved. I've a lot to tell you but it'll need to wait until we're back home." replied Kenny in a muted tone

"Harold came tae tell ye? Why am ah no likin the sound of this? Harold came to tell you? Oh fuck. What's going on?" Gus had turned paler than normal. Kenny looked at him and wondered if he should tell him the whole story but decided against it. Gus must have been in a hurry in the shower as he'd let the hair transplant get wet. It was now in a state of complete collapse having absorbed too much water. It looks like ginger seaweed draped across his scalp thought Kenny.

"Nothing we can do about it so come on, let's get into town and see what the story is." mumbled Kenny, trying to move the conversation back to a more comfortable topic

"Hey, were some guys no coming over on the ferry from Helsinki and Stockholm today. They'll be donald ducked if they don't know about it. Fuck me, what a game to miss" said Gus ruefully.

At that moment Gus was looking distinctly uncomfortable but Kenny didn't think it had anything to do with the earlier conversation about Harold.

"Have you got any o' that pile cream?" asked Gus "the Duke of Argylls are playing me up something rotten."

"Aye, its in my toiletry bag in the bog. Help yourself." replied Kenny.

Gus disappeared into the toilet for a minute before coming out looking a bit puzzled.

"Did you get it?" asked Kenny

"Yeah, its fine. I just don't understand why they need tae put mint in it," came the reply

""Mint?"

"Aye, it was smellin spearminty"

"Have you put your contact lenses in?"

"No, whats that got to do with anythin?"

"Because I think you've just pushed a finger full of toothpaste up your arse. Still, puts a new meaning on the term ring of confidence," said Kenny with a wry grin on his face.

"You bastard. This goes no further, right. ah've been the butt o' enough jokes on this trip, ah fuck, what did ah say that for, ach do what you want" cried Gus who looked like he was going to explode with frustration.

"Go on, brush your teeth with the Anusol for piles of smiles" came Kenny's reply.

"Look, come on" said Gus, "we've barely got three hours pre match drinkin time so get yer finger out, just like ah did a minute ago".

Kenny smoothed out the bed and sorted out his gear for the match on it. Unlike a lot of fans, he preferred to wear jeans to a game as opposed to a kilt. He knew the main attraction of the kilt for most guys was its attractiveness to the opposite sex but he had Alison and crap chat up technique. Besides even he knew the kilt wasn't going to do that much for him. Plus he was not the only person in the room suffering from Farmer Giles. A pair of jeans and a snug pair of boxers helped keep Kenny's piles under control and he was fucked if he was going to let the remote possibility of a shag mean he would be wandering round Tallinn with a sweaty arse. He also had to get his match kit ready and was taking into consideration the weather conditions. T-shirt under the top for this he thought and a jacket. He also found the Think Scottish baseball cap from the other night so stuck it on. He rounded it all off by tying a Lion Rampant flag round his neck in the form of a scarf.

"There you go, no quite the extra from Braveheart like some of youse but it'll have to do" he said as he looked in the mirror before going into the corridor to catch up with Gus. They made it downstairs in the lift only to find Harold waiting for them.

"Beat it, Gus, ah need a word in private wi Kenny." Harold issued his command with a curt nod of the head for Kenny to follow him into the coffee bar. Harold looked as if somebody might have rained on his parade and Kenny had a fair idea who that somebody might be. Gus had followed Harold's orders straight away and was now outside the hotel with a concerned look on his face, watching through the window as Harold broke some bad news to Kenny.

"Ah knew that wee shite Atholl or Andy or whatever the fuck he's called was a nasty wee piece o' work but it looks like ah never really impressed it enough on the boys. They got a bit cocky when they were puttin him in a laundry basket and turned their back on him for a minute too long. As o' now , Tony is in Tallinn A + E getting treatment for a broken nose, two black eyes and a fucked jaw, courtesy of Atholl smackin him in the puss with a fire extinguisher. Fortunately as he tried to do Alec he slipped on a pair of dirty tights and Alec was able to do the wee cunt first. The bad news is, this leaves us one man short for the job"

Kenny made a large mental leap to a very uncomfortable conclusion.

"Wait a minute, Harold, don't think I'm not grateful but come on. You don't mean you want me to......." stuttered Kenny.

"It's no a case of "want", mair like "need" ye to put in an appearance wi us this afternoon. As far as ah see it, ah've saved yer life this mornin and ye owe me, bigtime. In fact, had it not been for you, ah wouldnae be in this position o' being a man light on the biggest job of ma career so far. So from ma point of view, ye're in it up to your eyebrows, Kenny, and before you even think about saying "What about the game, Harold?" ah've no come all this way to call it off now because my son-in-law is worried about missin a poxy fucken football match. Be back here at 2pm on the dot."

* * * * *

Where had it all gone wrong, thought Atholl as he lay in the back of a Mercedes van, parked in the car park of the Grand Hotel. It wasn't meant to be like this but come on, pull yourself together. You've been in civvy street too long if you start thinking like that he told himself and tried to take a more positive viewpoint.

He had taken one of them out and if it hadn't been for that pair of tights causing him to slip on the wet tiles, he'd have taken care of the other one. Lucky amateurs or what! Still they'd given him a fair whack to the legs earlier on and that was one trick he would have to remember for the future.

To add insult to injury the pair of tights that had literally caused his downfall were now being used as a gag. Even more worryingly, despite the pain in his legs, his bound hands and ankles plus the throbbing at the back of his neck, it was another kind of throbbing which was now causing him concern. How on earth could he be getting turned on by a pair of dirty tights in his mouth, the state he was in? A stiffy in his state was unthinkable, especially as his body's position gave little or no room for manouevre for any kind of hard on. He had to admit they'd trussed him up like the proverbial Christmas turkey, binding his hands and ankles then using a pair of handcuffs to connect the two sets of rope. Thus, Atholl looked like he was touching his toes but at the same time, trying to find room for his penis to reach full maturity. Whoever had these tights before must have been one dirty bitch, thought Atholl as the taste brought back memories of a series of sexual encounters he'd previously managed to lose deep in his subconscious. He tried to remove all thoughts of sexiness from them by imagining their owner as some old Estonian crone who suffered from mild incontinence but it wasn't working. Still, at least the pain in his groin as his prick struggled for some space, like a mole trying to burrow through concrete, took some of the agony away from his legs. He also felt something odd around his ears when he moved his head. He couldn't put his finger on it but then his head touched the van panel and he realised what the weird feeling was. They had shaved his head completely!

The back door of the van opened and a man Atholl didn't recognise got in. His captors had made no effort to hide their faces so Atholl presumed this was it. He'd had a good innings, especially when his time in Northern Ireland was taken into consideration, so no complaints. Just a pity the chief would never know.

"Awright wee man?" came the voice drenched in a Glasgow accent. "Are we havin fun yet? Ye've caused me a wee bit of grief on a very important day in ma life Atholl and to put it mildly, its just not on. Ah would have been slightly upset if ye'd topped my son in law as he is, regrettably, family but to get in the way of business is somethin else. Then again Atholl, from what ah know about ye, ye're somethin else yourself."

All of a sudden Atholl's erection had vanished. How on earth did this piece of Glaswegian dogshit know his name? This was not right, not right at all.

"Anyway, come on. To show you ahm not all mean hearted ah've brought ye a wee drinky-poo. Nothing fancy like ye'd be drinkin in the Atlantic Bar or Quaglino's, but ah'm sure ye'll appreciate it enough."

Harold MacMillan produced a water bottle like the type used by cyclists on the Tour de France. He pulled the pair of tights in Atholl's mouth to one side and squirted the bottle hard. The liquid went up through the flexi straw and burst into his mouth. Atholl was reluctant to take the drink, but he'd been thrown by the fact the guy knew his real name and he was completely parched. Harold gave the bottle a couple of generous squeezes and the liquid dribbled down Atholl's chin where it had not been forced down his throat. "Oops silly me" said Harold. "Ah

166

should have said it'll be like the Atlantic bar cause ye've just had a wee cocktail. Sorry there wisnae a paper umbrella or a cherry wi it but where ye're goin ah don't think it would make much difference. Sweet dreams, wee Atholl, sweet dreams."

The fucker thought Atholl, the complete and utter fu..........

In the taxi into the centre of Tallinn Gus, had started to ask Kenny about his conversation with Harold but one look from Kenny had shut him up. Better keep schtum on this one he thought as Kenny looked totally pissed off. This was in stark contrast to the mood in the old town. Everywhere Scotland fans were running around telling other fans what they already knew. The game had been moved and the kick off was at 3 pm. Rumours were circulating over whether the Estonians would turn up or not. Some people thought they would, others believed there would definitely be no game. Nobody thought about asking any Estonians, as that would have been too obvious.

Kenny had bumped into a couple of Scots guys in their mid 40s in a café. He'd met them once before but had been hacked off by their patronising attitude. He also knew them to be jazz fans, which probably explained why they saw themselves as superior. These were the last people he wanted to meet at this moment in time. Gus, unaware of this, bounced up to them on entering the café and informed them the game had been moved to 3pm. He was casually informed they had known since 9 am and had already done a radio interview with a friend who worked at BBC Scotland.

"Just wanted to make sure you knew, like" he said before he turned back to Kenny, whilst making a face that showed just what he thought of them.

"Eh, I've got to go back to the hotel to help Harold with something. I'll see you at the game" said Kenny who got up and walked out of the café before Gus could say anything. Gus knew this was bad news but couldn't think of anything to do. He decided to find Dominic and take it from there.

* * * * *

Alec pulled up in front of the Hotel in the white Mercedes van at 2pm. Harold was in the passenger seat and when he saw Kenny he got out and let him take the seat in the front of the van. Harold stood with the van door in one hand and one hand on Kenny's shoulder.

"Now calm down, Kenny. We've got aw this sussed. Yer wee pal in the back has been a bit o' a fly in the ointment but as it turns oot, its not all bad news for us. For him, maybe but no for us, we'll just have to wait and see." At this Harold burst out laughing. "Ah've just seen a wee bit o' irony here. Ah don't know fuck all about football and here ah am, ahm goin to the game and you, one of Scotland's biggest fans is goin to miss it. Nae luck, son. See ye later."

Kenny had a rueful look on his face as Harold slammed the door shut and walked back into the hotel.

Alec put the van in gear and drove off. "Sorry, Kenny, it's nothing personal but if you don't play ball Harold says I've to pull you back in line. By any means. Ok?"

"Aye ok" whispered Kenny. "Why the fuck is he going to the game?"

"A small matter of an alibi, I do believe. He's bribed a newspaper photographer to make sure there will be a photae o him at the match in a Scottish daily tomorrow. Maybe no centre stage but somewhere in a wee corner where he can prove he was definitely at the game." replied Alec. "Look, when we get to the place just do as I say and it will be ok. Harold doesnae pull these stunts for a laugh and its all been nicely planned. Follow my orders and we'll be in and out in no time. Ok?"

"Aye, ok," came a muted reply.

Chapter 12

One Team in Tallinn

ALEC HAD LEFT the van radio on some local station before he had disappeared. The sound of the Fugees singing "Killing Me Softly" gently filled the van. There's fucking irony for you thought Kenny. Outside an old woman stood in the doorway of a dilapidated building holding out a cup. Kenny had been surprised at the number of elderly Estonians out begging. He wondered what the new post Soviet Union culture was like for the old fuckers, how did you survive a crash course in capitalism at the age of 78? Two kids came running down the street one of them wearing a Juventus top, shouting something in Estonian at his mate. Kenny was reminded of the Jam song "Dreams of Children". All he knew was that he was definitely going underground once this caper was over. He sat in the van and wondered how the fuck it had come to this. It looked likely that in the space of 24 hours he would survive an attempt on his life, take part in a criminal offence, sorry, a serious criminal offence and to cap it all, miss the one game that people would be talking about for years to come. He turned round in his seat and looked at Andy or Atholl or whoever he was. What have I done to you to deserve all this you bastard?

"Ok, game on" said Alec as he appeared at the passenger window. He was wearing a collar and tie, sunglasses and a well cut pin stripe suit.

"What the fuck are you doing dressed like that?" demanded Kenny.

"Get real Kenny, for fucks sake. What wir ye expectin? A black mask, a hooped jumper an a bag wi "swag" written oan it? Get wi the project, right?". He turned his head back down the van and shouted "Martin, now".

Kenny turned his head out of the passenger window to see a tall well built man in a suit similar to Alec's get out of a Mercedes saloon parked behind Kenny's van. He was also wearing a collar and tie and sunglasses. Behind him two guys dressed in painter and decorators overalls got out of a beaten up van. As he was looking a smaller guy also got out of the Merc, again sharply dressed in a business suit.

"Ok, here's how it's goin doon, Kenny. Me, Leo and Martin here are casually goin in tae the bank and wir goin tae the safe deposit room. The two painters are going tae take Atholl in wi us, wrapped up in a sheet. There'll be a wee bit o a kerfuffle as they're no expected so then we make oor move. We dae what we have to dae and then come back out again, nice as ninepence, leaving Sleeping Beauty in there tae face the music."

The bigger of the two locals, Martin, approached the van. "Everything A ok?" he asked.

"Nae problem big man" said Alec. "Kenny here is the eyes of the operation and if anythin looks like it will go tits up, he'll blow the horn."

171

"Tits up? Blow the horn? You crazy Scots guys always thinking about pussy" came the reply from Martin, who had a big grin on his face.

"No, that's the last thing on ma mind at this moment in time, ah can assure you," said Alec, "No time for fannyin about o any kind now. Lets go."

The painters slid open the side door of the van and proceeded to wrap Atholl in a dust sheet. Kenny was a bit surprised to see Atholl also was wearing a good suit with a collar and tie as well, exactly the same as Leo. His head was completely shaved. The best dressed impersonation of Kojak I've ever seen thought Kenny. What the fuck was going on?

Alec took one last look round and said "Remember Kenny, eyes and ears ok. Ah've jist realised, this goes well enough, ye might even make the second half" He winked at Kenny and headed off across the street with the two well dressed Estonians. The painters slammed the side door shut and headed off carrying a neatly wrapped sausage roll with an Atholl filling on their shoulders.

The next twenty minutes were the longest of Kenny's life. The radio station was now playing "Three Lions on His Shirt" by Baddiel and Skinner. This just gets better and better he thought. The old woman was still in the doorway. Could she be a police undercover agent, waiting to call in some elite squad of Tallinn cops? Where had that boy in the Juve top gone? Could he be a Jimmy Clitheroe type waiting to pounce with a .44 Magnum hidden under his baggy top? His paranoia was getting too much for him and this music wasn't helping any. He would turn the radio off but he didn't have a clue how to do it. Knowing his luck he'd turn on the emergency lights, triggering the van alarm at the same time. He kept his eyes peeled for any sign of a police car or security staff but there was no flashing lights, no sirens and best of all no alarm bells.

Despite his state of high anxiety, he found himself looking disbelievingly as Alec and Martin, plus the two painters casually strolled across the road from the bank. What he didn't understand was why the painters were carrying the same bundle as before they had gone in? Where was the wee guy in the suit that had gone in with Martin and Alec? Where was the swag bag?

Alec climbed into the drivers seat and turned to Kenny with a big smile on his face, "Awright big boy? Ye did terrific pal, really great. Ye might jist hae found yourself an openin in the business. Once Tony can actually see out of his eyes again, he might find his position under threat. Harold's always looking' to add to his squad. Do you fancy a three year contract? The win bonuses won't always be guaranteed like this one but you never know." Alec burst out laughing but Kenny failed to see any humour in the situation.

As Alec was talking the two guys in the painters get up had climbed into the back of the van and had gently laid down the bundle they were carrying.

Kenny's eyes bulged as he saw Leo, the smaller of original three suited guys clamber out of the dust sheets. As he sat up he cried "Why the fuck are we still here? Let's go!!"

Alec put the van in gear and headed off. "No problem Leo".

"Could someone please tell me what the fuck is going on and why this seems to have passed off so easily?" asked Kenny in a bewildered tone of voice.

"Take it easy, Kenny" said Alec "Everythin's goin to be fine.

As far as the cameras are concerned three robbers went into the bank and two left. Unfortunately the third was clubbed by the security guard and sadly for him, had to be left behind."

"So where is it then? " asked Kenny

"What? The swag bag?" asked Alec in mocking tone.

"Don't fuck me about, Alec, you know what I mean"

"Calm down, Kenny, everythin's under control. We've got nothin on us as we've stolen nothin fae the bank." Alec took his right arm off the steering wheel and placed his hand on Kenny's knee.

"No way. We've been through this fucken charade and you're going to tell me you've done nothing but leave that wee bastard Atholl in the vault?" protested Kenny, a definite note of hysteria creeping into his voice.

"Look, we've slightly re-arranged things. Atholl turning up is a peach as it diverts attention fae us. They have a collar and we're away from it all the morn wi the rest of you football guys. "Scot free" you could say," Alec burst out laughing at his own joke.

"I'm still no gettin it" said Kenny.

"Look, it's a long story but tae cut tae the chase, Leo here owns the bank."

"He what? He's just robbed his own bank?" shouted Kenny struggling to comes to terms with what he was hearing. He turned round to look at Leo who was undoing his tie. Leo gave Kenny a very laid back grin.

"Aye, it's his bank. How can ye launder dodgy money if ye huvnae got a washin machine? Yesterday he took delivery of two million quids worth of diamonds fae the mines in Siberia en route tae Antwerp. We've gaun in an moved things aboot so it looks like somebody has trousered the gear, when in fact it's in a safe deposit box a few drawers along, owned by Harold. He set it up a few months ago on his first visit out here. We've smashed a few boxes open and thrown stuff about. Normal villainy, eh?. Leo's goat insurance and we've goat the diamonds. Get what I'm saying? We've left Atholl in there wi a belt round the lughole from the security guards truncheon and when he comes round or rather down, he'll be able to tell them fuck all."

"Harold's been here before? What do you mean when he comes down?" asked Kenny. He couldn't keep up.

"Harold made him one of his special cocktails before we went in. Two thirds LSD and one third sleeping tablets. When he wakes up he'll be seein lizards and Betty Boo crawlin up his cell wall. Good luck to the cunt as its more than he deserves."

"But really, you're telling me I've been used," cried Kenny. "Harold didn't need any cover or any help at all. He's already been here! Unbe-fucking-lievable!"

"Take it up wi him when you see him, Kenny. Ahm sure he'll understand your point of view. He's an easygoing kinda guy." Alec was smiling from ear to ear. Kenny turned round to see Leo trying not to laugh too much at Kenny's frustrated cries of outrage.

They were now approaching the old docks. Kenny had been through this area in 1994 when he got off the ferry from Helsinki. It was being modernised but there were still a few areas of grim warehouses where it would be unwise to go without a formal welcome.

Alec pulled the van into a large vaulted warehouse. Two men were waiting for them and as Alec and Kenny got out, along with the three guys in the back, they jumped in and drove off. As they were driving off, Kenny noticed for the first time the van had Latvian number plates.

"Not a bad wee tickle as it happens. What do you reckon Kenny?" asked Alec, a broad smile on his face. "Want to say thank you thank you to Leo for arrangin aw this? In a roundabout way he's saved your life as if it wasnae fur him, we wouldnae be here and you know where that would have left you, don't you?"

"Aye, lyin on the floor of a sauna wonderin why it was so cold," replied Kenny. "Somehow, I think I'll pass on the thank yous until I'm safely back home."

"Alright. Have it your way, you fucking Dumfries ingrate". Kenny suddenly looked at Alec as he had normally been friendly towards him. Alec broke into a big smile and said "Just a wee wind up, Kenny, take it easy. As Liam Gallagher says "Don't Look Back in Anger". You'll still make the second half. Come on we'll give you a lift up the street and you can get a taxi to the stadium."

Chapter 13

Post Match Round Up

KENNY GOT OUT of the taxi at the park and wandered up towards the Kadriorg Stadium. It was 3.30 and he was a bit puzzled to see a stream of people walking towards him, all of whom appeared to be Scots. He saw Gus and Dominic both of whom looked rather hot and sweaty for some bizarre reason.

"Well hello stranger!" said Gus "have you missed yourself or what? Fuckin' Estonians never showed up, man. Doddsy passed it to Collins and the ref blew the whistle. Ye just had tae be there."

"What happened Kenny or can you no say?" quizzed Dominic in a low voice. "Gus said you'd been speaking to Harold."

"Got held up at the bank, if you must know. I'll tell you later. Why are you two so fucking sweaty? Don't tell me there's been more group sex in the changing rooms," Kenny was trying to lighten the mood but it was a sore one.

"Nah, better than group sex. We've just had the kickaboot tae end all kickaboots. After the team went off, this fat wee ugly guy in a kilt ran on to the pitch with a ball from the touchline, dummied a security guard and slotted the ball home. Cue mass invasion by Scotland fans. Ah nearly scored but was taken out by some cunt from Burntisland. It was absolutely magic." He'd never known Gus to take uppers but Kenny could swear he was high on something now.

Kenny looked at them both and they looked radiant. Dominic was absolutely crap at football but he'd still got on and it had made the trip for him. The lack of a game wasn't an issue as they'd both been there. Scotland would get the three points for one kick of the ball but more importantly these guys had been at an event that would echo round the world of football for years to come. He'd missed it. He was alive but he'd still missed being there. What a complete and utter bummer. Whoever said life was more important than football had got it wrong.

"Everythin' alright wi Harold?" Gus asked, a concerned note in his voice.

"Aye, sweet as a nut. Everything's sorted." said Kenny. "I think I'll go up and have a look so that at least I can say I was in the ground. I'll catch you back in the pub. What one are you's going to?"

"Hell Hunt as per usual. The Nimita will be mobbed" repled Dominic.

"Ok, catch you in there." muttered Kenny as he turned away.

Kenny continued his walk up to the ground. It was a trickle of fans that were coming out now and most of the fans looked a combination of delirious and knackered. The average consumption of alcohol by a fan before a game went against having a mass kickabout five minutes after kick off when most people expected to be still queuing to get in. He was able to walk into the ground without showing a ticket as they'd opened the gates to let the fans out. He was astonished to see there were still some people on the pitch until he realised it was the Scotland squad going through a training routine.

Pa Broon was out there shouting at them as was, Alex Miller. Wonder if he's still got the ice cream van pondered Kenny. Paul, a friend of Kenny's, had grown up on an estate near Clydebank where Alex Miller had an ice cream van round when he was playing for Rangers. Kenny's mate was a Celtic fan and had enjoyed a good bit of banter with Miller. In the early 70s Miller had scored an absolute screamer in the last minute if an Old Firm game at Pakhead to win the match 2-1 for Rangers. Paul told him that Miller was still out in the van later on that night doing his rounds, winding Paul up despite the fact he was the toast of the blue half of Glasgow.

He was watching the squad go through its paces when a familiar voice called "Mr Bradley, still here I see." Kenny turned round to see Frances Fairweather walking up to him with a quizical expression on her face.

"No, just got here Frances". The words were out of his mouth before he could stop himself. Oh fuck, shouldn't have said. Frances had been a teacher before joining the SFA and he knew straight away she could smell out a lie the way Gus could smell out a slapper.

"Just got here? And why is that? Don't tell me you missed all the action?" she said, her eyes fixing a steely gaze on his.

"Yes, one of those things. Forgot my ticket, had to go back to the hotel and then got caught in traffic. Did I miss much?"

"From a footballing point of view, no, but you did miss the Scotland fans serenading me when I was making an announcement over the tannoy."

"Oh aye, what was it? Flower of Scotland? A wee bit of Neil Diamond?" asked Kenny with a smile on his face.

"No, it was that well known Scottish ballad that goes something like" and here Frances took a deep breath to gently sing "get yer tits out, get yer tits out, get yer tits out for the lads, get yer tits out for the lads".

Kenny burst out laughing.

"I saw Mr McSween singing it quite lustily so tell him that I am looking forward to him giving me a personal serenade soon. I never realised he was such a chanteuse." Frances had a mischievous look on her face.

"I'll be sure to mention it to him" said Kenny.

"But what about you Kenny, is everything ok in your life?"

Ah, the classic Frances Fairweather sting. Lull you into a false sense of security and then get you right in the guts with a swift upper hook. He knew she didn't believe a word he'd been saying but there was no way he was telling her what had just happened that afternoon.

"Never better Frances" replied Kenny "never better. Six points from two games, two clean sheets and a memorable day in Tallinn all round. Can't complain. Think I'll be heading back into town. You flying back tonight?"

"Yes. Once they've finished this session, we're off. And yourself?"

"The morn's mornin."

"You flying back with your father-in-law? I saw he was at the game. I thought you might have told me he'd become a bit of a Scotland fan with him joining the supporters club as well."

Oh fuck, he was on the ropes now, he'd taken the earlier body blow but she was going for a knockout with that last comment.

"I expect so but Harold's a bit of a law unto himself, if you get my drift" he managed to reply. "Well is that the time? I've got to go and meet the rest of the guys, so have a safe flight home and I'll be in touch."

"You take care Kenny. Have a safe flight" Frances had that knowing look on her face yet again and Kenny couldn't get out of that park quick enough.

He caught a cab to the Hell Hunt and immediately regretted it. This was the first western style pub opened in Tallinn after the Estonians gained their independence. It had been decorated in mock Irish pub style but at that moment in time looked more like a mock Irish funeral parlour. The late afternoon gloom from outside was being absorbed by the dark, heavy Irish furniture. To make matters worse Christy Moore singing some dirge like Irish ballad was playing through the pub's sound system. Gus and Dominic sat at a table, two empty bowls in front of them. Kenny had expected a few more fans to be in but it was deadly quiet. Kenny looked at his two pals and realised the adrenaline of this afternoon's events had vanished. They both looked quietly contemplative and Kenny's appearance seemed to wake them from some kind of trance.

"Awright Kenny?" asked Gus "we've just been talkin about you funnily enough".

Dominic shot Gus an angry glance but Gus ploughed on. "We can't work out what you've been up to and we don't want to know. All we're saying is, like, that we're here for you pal. If Harold and his heavies want to start anything, they'll have to get past Dominic and me first".

This was all said with a confident tone but Kenny knew the

facts of the matter. Gus and Dominic couldn't fight sleep so God knows what Alec, Martin or Leo would do to them.

"Calm down for fucks sake. You've been watching too many kamikaze films on Bravo. It's all sorted and nothing else is going to happen to us from Harold."

"Oh aye" said Dominic with a quzzical tone. He nodded at a TV in the corner "Can you explain that to us then?". The screen showed the front of the bank where Kenny had been parked earlier on. A couple of police cars were parked outside with the lights on the roof flashing merrily away. Two policemen were standing outside the entrance to the bank and another two had just left carrying Atholl McClackit between them. The three fans looked at the screen transfixed as Atholl appeared to try to point to something then shrieked with laughter. Another policeman came from behind and grabbed his ear to try and control his head. By the time he'd got a grip Atholl had calmed down and appeared to have passed out. The screen then cut away to newsreader sitting behind a desk.

She continued reading the news about the diamond robbery with a still photo of Atholl being held by two policemen, hovering just above her right shoulder.

Dominic asked the barman what the news report was about. The barman turned the TV up and listened intently. He then put his lips together and blew out a small whistle.

"Big diamond robbery at bank. 50 million kroon in diamonds taken by thieves. Guy in photo captured by security. He face long jail time"

Gus and Dominic turned to Kenny, bewildered expressions on their faces but all he could say was "Don't ask, just don't fucking ask, ok?"

Chapter 14

Game Over

KENNY WAS STANDING in Tallinn airport's duty free shop trying to work out what perfume to get Alison. The shop wasn't much more than an enlarged kiosk and the range was pretty small. His mind was all over the shop as the events of the last week raced around in his brain. He felt a presence standing next to him and turned to see Harold MacMillan standing before him with a big smile on his face. Behind Harold was Alec, a knowing grin on his face and next to him Tony. Well he thought it was Tony. There were so many bandages on his face Kenny had difficulty identifying him. Atholl must have caught him good style with that fire extiguisher thought Kenny. Looking back to Harold, Kenny could see his false eye was glistening somewhat and for some reason he had this bizarre image of Harold putting eye drops in his false eye.

"Alright, Kenny. Never had you doon for the Chanel type masel. A bit too classy for you, is it no?" teased Harold. He had caught Kenny in what could loosely be described the Chanel section of the duty free shop in that Kenny was standing next to the one shelf containing the one bottle of Chanel No 5.

"Fortunately it's no for me, Harold, it's for Alison. I think you might be a wee bit disappointed yourself mind."

"Oh aye, how's that?"

"They seem to be out of Brut 33"

"Very fuckin funny. Just as well ahm in a good mood wi ye at this moment in time. Ah heard ye didnae let the boys doon so ah've got a wee memento fur ye."

"A diamond? Oh Harold, you shouldn't have. People will talk. I'm a married man" replied Kenny a big grin on his face.

"Will ye do the right thing for once and just shut the fuck up. Here, ahm almost tempted no to gie it to ye now but ye've done ok considerin you're a lippy cunt." Harold shoved a carrier bag in to Kenny's chest. Kenny opened the bag and found himself looking at a Scotland top. Not any Scotland top but one worn by one of the players the previous day. There was a number on the back and the SFA badge was embroidered into the material.

Kenny was stunned. He'd always wanted a genuine top but the prices had gone through the roof as the football memorabilia market took off.

"Where did you get this?" he asked Harold.

"One o the players was gettin in a bit too deep at ma casino. Ah told him ah wouldd look kindly on his debts if he could come up wi a top fur me. When its yer achilles tendon or a poxy bit of 100% polyester eh, it does focus the mind a wee bit? Just hope it fits. It's no exactly goin fae one athletic frame to another, is it?"

"Eh, aye, you're right there. Thanks a million, Harold. If there's anything I can ever..." Kenny's voice trailed off as he realised what he was saying.

"Don't worry, Kenny. Ah didnae get where ah am takin unnecessary chances. Once is enough for you, as far as ahm concerned. Have a safe flight home. Ye goin via Copenhagen?"

"Aye, what about you? You no doing the same?"

"No, ah've got a couple of business opportunities croppin up in Moscow with Leo so we're goin to visit some acquaintances there before it gets too nippy. Ah'll be back home at the weekend so tell Alison ah'll see her on Monday mornin. Ok?"

"Aye, ok. Take care." Kenny was relieved to see Harold walk away towards the boarding gate for the Moscow flight. As he turned away with Harold, Alec made a gun out of his right hand and pointed it at Kenny. He had a big smile on his face all the while. Kenny grinned back at him. As for what Tony was doing with his face, Kenny had no idea, but hoped it was painful. Miserable fuck.

Kenny looked up at the departures screen only to realise he still had another 45 minutes before the SAS flight to Copenhagen was due to leave. Kenny was wondering what to tell Alison when he got home but decided silence was the only option. She'd probably find out about his adventures when Harold turned up at work with six million Estonian kroons and asked her to take it down Thomas Cook's for a decent rate of exchange.

He looked around the departure terminal and saw Gus trying to chat up the girl working the till in the cafeteria. As he approached Gus, Kenny saw he was just in time to see her give him a piece of paper

"Come on you, can you not give it a rest for five minutes" Kenny sighed.

"These burds love me man, its in ma endolphins or ma

fairygnomes, one or the other." boasted Gus as he pocketed the bit of paper. He blew a kiss to the girl on the till and she giggled. They walked off towards the seated area to await the call for their flight.

"What happened to the one in the blue dress last night?" asked Kenny.

"No problem. Clinched the deal back at hers, like."

"She was pretty good looking apart from those boils on her arm," replied Kenny, a trace of a smile playing on his face.

"For the last time they werenae boils, it was a nervous condition," claimed an exasperated sounding Gus.

"Well that's understandable."

"What de ye mean by that?" asked Gus.

"Well I'd definitely be nervous if I was going to shag you. They might come in handy those boils you know. You run out of KY jelly, you just pop a boil and there's your lubricant."

"Aw get tae fuck man. That is one of the most disgustin' things I've ever heard. You're one sick bastard Bradley, you really fucking are." Gus' face contorted as he thought back to what Kenny had said.

In an effort to regain the high ground, Gus continued "What we had last night was beautiful, like, a man and a woman doing the most natural thing in the world and you've got to spoil it for me, like. The poetic beauty of life just passes you by at times pal. You're a bitter, bitter man, Kenny Bradley."

"Oh fuck off, "what we had last night was the poetic beauty of life" you're having a laugh. If it was so beautiful how long did you stay after you had sex. 5 minutes, 15 minutes or did you push the boat out and stay for half an hour's post coital pillow talk?"

Gus had a resigned look on his face.

"Ok smart bastart, it wasnae quite five minutes but there was mitigatin circumstances, like. She lives wi her mother in one o those Russian built estates, no hot water, black and white telly that sort of thing. She normally shares the bed wi the mother so when we get in, we're getting down to it on the rug in front of the fire like. Everything's goin well, till the family dog appears from nowhere and starts lickin ma arse. Now ah've had a few funny experiences on the job in my time, burds sticking their middle finger up ma ring, that sort of thing, but nothin like this dog. It had some tongue on it by the way. So this is really gettin me goin, you know what ah mean like"

"No, sorry. As I've never had a dog lick my arse whilst I've been having sex, I don't quite know what you mean, but do continue. I suppose it puts a new meaning into the term doing it "doggy style"" said Kenny who was struggling to believe what he was hearing.

"Aye aye, ok, don't get clever, so there ah am in full stride like, a real buckin bronco, givin it laldy and this dog's tongue is the biggest turn on ah've ever had like. So you know what happens. I shoot ma load, start mooin like a cow and this dog goes absolutely mental. The burds right into what we're doin but then realises the dog will wake her mother up. She puts her hand over my mouth to shut me up but this just gets me goin even worse. Then the bedroom door opens and the old crone comes out to see what's goin on. Fuckin bedlam ensues like, wi the dog barkin, the mother pullin me off the daughter and the poor wee lassie trying to cover hersel up. So that's me donald ducked in more than one sense ah can tell you. One minute ahm havin the best sex of my life courtesy of a dog lickin ma arse, the next minute I'm gettin barked at by the dog and huckled oot the door by the lassie's old dear."

"So did you get her number?"

"Who? The mother?"

"No, did you get Lassie's number"

"Aye, ah got it in the nightclub"

"That's no quite the Lassie I was thinking of. I know you've been out with a few dogs in your time but this is a new one to me. There's never been one that's licked your arse."

"Aw, get tae fuck. That's no funny ya mad bastard."

"You really are incredible at times. Dragging Dominic into it as well, that boy will never be the same." Kenny was shaking his head in disapproval.

"Aye right. He didnae look too unhappy at breakfast when I saw him last. I think he might even be meetin her fae last night later on. He's no flyin back till tomorrow, like."

Kenny thought back to the previous night's events. After they had left the Hell Hunt they had made their way through the old town square to the Nimita bar. The place was jumping with Scotland fans who couldn't believe what they had experienced. A crowd of Estonian fans had come into the bar but had quickly left as the whole bar sang at them "Where were you at three o'clock?" and "One team in Tallinn, there's only one team in Tallinn".

Kenny had spotted two women in a corner, one of whom was a bit of a looker in a blue dress but her pal looked like a million dollars, in loose change.

Gus had charged straight in but had hit a major stumbling block in that the girl in the blue dress spoke no English and it was clear her pal, who did speak English wasn't going to play the role of interpreter without a bit of male company herself. Luckily for Kenny he had been paying a visit to the gents when this had initially kicked off and, in a time of emergency, Gus had to endure Dominic in the role of wingman. Gus was paying a high price for his companionship. It was only the promise of free lager all night which ensured Dominic's continued attendance

Kenny had come back to the surreal sight of the four of them sitting round the table, with Gus saying to Dominic "Get her tae ask her what she does", Dominic then asking Anna what her friend does for a living in English and Anna asking her friend in the blue dress who was called Svea, the question in Estonian. Svea would say something to Anna who would then tell Dominic, who would then say "Gym instructor" to Gus. It was one of the most pathetic sights Kenny had ever seen so he went off looking for somebody to talk to about the days events and he didn't mean a bank robbery.

Gus had bounded into the room around 4 am commenting that, like Santa Claus on Boxing Day, his sacks were well and truly empty. Kenny had asked about Dominic but all Gus had done was cackle in an evil manner, then made some comment about "sending a boy to do a man's job" before falling on his bed, fully clothed and passing out.

They were called for the flight to Copenhagen. The whole plane was full of Scotland fans trying to put their brains back in order. A few were sporting Russian military caps and hats bought in the Tallinn flea market. I bet Gorby never thought he was going to set up an international market in military memorabilia when he brought the iron curtain down reflected Kenny. A couple of guys had gone the whole hog and bought jackets with medals to accompany the hats.

They boarded the plane and Gus had no sooner sat down than yet again he passed out. Kenny sat back and looked out at the clouds below them. The Baltic was occasionally visible through gaps in the steely grey clouds but there was nothing to see below. He thought back over the events of the last six days thinking this had been the trip to end all trips. He was still at a loss as to why Atholl or Andy or whoever had tried to kill him. He'd never ever heard of the guy. Maybe Harold could get a bit more info for him but he hoped he would be seeing less rather than more of Harold over the next few months. So, considering the last few days, he's seen Scotland win once, the U21's were undefeated in two games, he'd missed a game people would be talking about for years to come, somebody had tried to kill him, twice, if he thought back to Riga. He'd taken part in a diamond robbery where the diamonds hadn't left the bank and he'd got a genuine player's top.

All of a sudden he felt a surge of anger. The hotel electrics in Riga. He'd told that wee bastard Atholl they were dodgy and he'd legged it out of the bar not five minutes later. To think Jock Paisley died because of the wee shite. He couldn't be certain but it all made sense now, all the drinks on expenses, my God, maybe even Tadger Currie was murdered by him. Kenny was struggling to come to terms with what he'd just realised. He ran through what he could put together. The question that came back to haunt him was from Harold. How many Scotland fans normally die on trips? He couldn't pin Tadger Currie's demise on Atholl in the same way as Jock's but the wee bastard had definitely been in the bar prior to Tadger pegging it. Whatever was happening to Atholl, it wasn't enough in Kenny's book. He hadn't liked to ask Harold what the law would do to him but he hoped it was grim.

Gus was still fast asleep when all of a sudden he awoke with a start exclaiming, "Ma photaes, ma fuckin photaes" and immediately Kenny realised what he meant. With the excitement of the previous day, Gus had forgotten about his 3 pm appointment with the lady from the photo lab. At the time he was due to meet her, Gus had been standing in the Kadriorg singing "get your tits out for the lads" as Frances Fairweather made an announcement to the Scotland fans asking for calm.

"Looks like you'll just have to arrange another trip to Tallinn then Gus" said Kenny.

Gus's face relaxed into a smile as he said, "Could be an idea big boy, could be an idea."

* * * * *

Dair McClackit tied the last French tricolour round Sally McChisholm's ankle and the post of his bed. He had his Napoleon outfit on and had tried to tie her up as he would have imagined the man himself would have until he realised it was a physical impossibility with only one arm. Fortunately for Sally she was lying face down on the bed so she couldn't see his embarrassment. Fortunately for Dair, she was also stark naked and he was looking forward to a good afternoon's entertainment.

"Are you finished Dair?" she asked with an impatient tone. He had taken ten minutes to tie the last two, starting off using only one arm as a kind of experiment, till he realised it was taking too long and the effect of his pills might start to wane. Her earlier gentle snores had also been a bit of a prompt for him to hurry up.

"Sally, how many times have I told you it's Napoleon when I'm in uniform, not Dair," he said with an exasperated tone of voice.

"Sorry, mon general but is there any chance of Napoleon wielding his grande baguette this side of Christmas? I've got high tea with the rural at 5pm so if you don't allez vite we're going to have to call a halt just when its getting good."

"Ok, we're all set, I'll just put the tape on" Sally sighed heavily.

"Do we have to Dair, sorry Napoleon. Just for once, I would like to have sex without the 1812 Overture blaring in my ear."

"Calm down, Sally. It all adds to the effect. I just have to hit the play button.

Dair McClackit was halfway across the bedroom when there was a knock on the door. He'd told Potter he was not to be disturbed under any circumstances. The man knew better than to interrupt him when he was with Sally McChisholm.

"Yes, Potter. What is it?" he bellowed across the room.

"A phone call sir, master Atholl, it's most urgent." came the muted reply through the door.

"Wait a minute" shouted Dair as he walked across the room. He had been in numerous battles with Potter who had served him loyally for 40 years and there was little they didn't know about each other. However, this Napoleon get up was a bit of an embarrassment, despite their comradeship so Dair took his cocked hat off and opened the door just enough to take the phone. He picked up the receiver and held it to his ear

"Atholl? Atholl, what's wrong. Why are you crying, Atholl? Atholl? What's happened? What have they done to you"

Printed in the United Kingdom
by Lightning Source UK Ltd.
124495UK00001B/208/A